"You are driving very well indeed, Miss Penrose. You have many hidden talents."

Araminta interrupted her concentration to steal a glance at him. "They are not in the least remarked upon in a gentleman. Moreover, it is most vexing when a female endowed with great beauty is not expected to possess any further qualities, whereas a female who is positively plain is required to be stupid, too!"

"I hope you do not refer to yourself, for plainspoken you may be, but plain you most definitely are not!"

She caught her breath and turned to look at him in amazement, only for him to reach out and grab the reins to avoid a collision with a loaded cart.

THE DUKE'S DILEMMA

Rachelle Edwards

FAWCETT CREST • NEW YORK

A Fawcett Crest Book
Published by Ballantine Books
Copyright © 1992 by Rachelle Edwards

All rights reserved under International and Pan-American Copyright Conventions. Published in the United States by Ballantine Books, a division of Random House, Inc., New York, and simultaneously in Canada by Random House of Canada Limited, Toronto.

Library of Congress Catalog Card Number: 91-92395

ISBN 0-449-22123-7

Manufactured in the United States of America

First Edition: June 1992

ONE

Oliver Barrington, Duke of Avedon, reined in his horse on the brow of a hill. As the big chestnut stallion skittered to a halt, the duke sat back in the saddle and surveyed Summerhills, his magnificent Elizabethan mansion, with a great feeling of satisfaction.

Countless diamond-paned windows glinted in the afternoon sun, and shadows began to lengthen across the lawns, set out by Capability Brown half a century earlier to replace an old ornate Elizabethan garden. Only a small knot garden remained, gazed upon from the drawing room, and reached from the terrace. Once left in neglect, it had been restored to its former glory where peacocks roamed once again, squawking their raucous noise.

On every single occasion he approached Summerhills from this direction after a day on his estate, the duke experienced a similar feeling of satisfaction, made more acute by the knowledge of how close he had come to losing it all.

After those few minutes of reflection, he spurred on his horse and galloped down the hill, startling a grazing herd of deer as he plowed past them. He galloped into the stable yard, and just as he dismounted, a traveling carriage rattled into it, too.

The duke glanced at it curiously before he strode toward the house to confront the visitor.

On entering the great hall, he tossed his hat at the house steward, and his valet hurried forward to assist him. The great hall was the original hub of the house. It still retained the massive fireplace where oxen were roasted in the time of the first duke. Once the household dined at a huge table in that very hall, but no more. The paneled walls remained as they always were, as did the massive iron chandelier, which was lowered each day to replace and to light the many candles it contained.

The moment the duke sank into the leather porter's chair, his valet began to pull off his dusty boots.

"Who's my visitor? Not Lady Stanyon, I trust. That would be more than flesh and blood could endure after a day of estate business!"

The valet allowed himself a small smile, aware of his master's aversion to any visitor, let alone one of his sisters. "It is Master . . . Mister Turlington, Your Grace."

The duke looked startled at the mention of his ward. "Hal? What the devil is Hal Turlington doing at Summerhills after all these years? I hope the cub isn't in the suds."

"Mr. Turlington seemed to be in high snuff, Your Grace, and merely intimated an overdue desire to see you," the house steward informed him.

Properly shod, the duke stood up again and straightened to his full six feet of height. "Where is he? In the library availing himself of my Armagnac, I suppose?"

"No, Your Grace. After I acquainted him with

2

the dinner hour, Mr. Turlington elected to go directly to his room to rest after the journey."

"My stars! Resting in the afternoon at his age. I shall be obliged to restrain my curiosity until dinner, but at least the Armagnac is safe for now."

Precisely an hour later, the duke, having bathed away the grime of the day and attired for dinner, came down the great staircase once trod, rumor had it, by Queen Elizabeth herself. Rumor also told that the first duke was the Queen's lover, but there was no confirmation of the fact and nothing to be divined from the Knollys portrait of him that hung at the head of the stairs, save for the enigmatic smile on the darkly handsome face.

When the duke entered the small drawing room, his ward, Henry Turlington, was already waiting for him, standing in front of a portrait of another Avedon ancestor with his hands clasped behind his back. As the footman closed the door behind the duke, the young man turned to smile at his guardian. The duke was somewhat taken aback at the sight of this fashionably attired young man, who wore a broadcloth coat of blue superfine with broad shoulders and nipped-in waist. His shirt collar was, to the duke's eyes, ludicrously high and threatened to cut the boy's ears, but he suspected he was clad in the height of fashion—although he could not be certain, so long had it been since he had mixed in fashionable circles himself. Just then he felt it had been far too long, for the once tousled-headed boy now sported his hair in a fashionably curled and pomaded style.

"Your Grace!" the young man greeted his guardian, coming forward with outstretched hand.

3

"Hal, how you've grown" was all the duke could say as they shook hands.

"The boy has become a man, eh?"

"A very handsome one, too."

The young man's face became a little flushed, which indicated he hadn't been a man for so very long. "Forgive me for coming with no prior warning."

"Not at all. You need no invitation to visit me, now or in the future. I believed that was understood between us."

"I am very much obliged to you," the young man replied, looking more than a little relieved. "I trust I find you in good health," he ventured a moment later.

"Yes, you need harbor no doubts on that score. I trust that all is well at Mapplewood."

"Oh, Lord, yes. Everything is fine."

Satisfied, the duke then went to a small table and poured two glasses of Madeira from a decanter standing there. He returned a few moments later, handed one glass to his handsome ward, and then indicated a chair at the side of the fireplace.

When they were seated, the duke said, "I hope you're comfortable here, Hal. Summerhills can be devilishly drafty to those accustomed to more manageable houses."

"Oh, indeed I am, Your Grace. In fact, I'm delighted to see Summerhills looking so fine after hearing reports of its decline."

The duke smiled faintly. "I'm aware that the difficulties my family was undergoing a few years ago were well known abroad."

"Your situation, as I observe it now, does you much credit."

4

The duke raised his glass. "A toast to you, Hal. I am proud of you. I read all your reports from Oxford with much pleasure. You did very well, and somehow avoided the temptations of dissipating your time there. Now, tell me, what brings you to Summerhills after all this time?"

For a moment the young man looked slightly uncomfortable before he recovered himself to say, "If you will not deem to come to London or Mapplewood to see Mama and I, I decided it was well past the time I called upon *you*."

The older man put down his glass. "You're quite correct, of course. I have, in my ardor to restore Summerhills to its former glory, neglected my duties as a guardian."

"I have always understood your difficulties, but be certain I hold you in enormous respect, and I am immensely proud of having you as my guardian. After Father died, I recall you were most kind and attentive, to Mama as well as myself."

The duke smiled wryly. "But a mite neglectful since. However, I am determined to rectify that omission in the future. There are, after all, several years left until you come into your inheritance."

Mr. Turlington looked none too pleased at the promise, and continued to concentrate on his drink.

"I half suspected you might be a little embarrassed for blunt," the duke ventured. "which would be nothing out of the ordinary for a young man of your age."

The young man smiled almost scornfully. "Oh no, Your Grace, I am always up in the stirrups." The duke's eyebrows rose slightly as Mr. Turlington added, rather pompously his guardian thought, "I do not fall into the traps that await young men just down from Oxford."

While the duke considered his ward carefully, he could find no real cause for criticism. Hal Turlington was studying his guardian in a similar fashion. It was something of a relief to discover the duke much as he recalled, despite some of the alarming rumors that were circulating. His guardian was as imposing a man as he had appeared when Hal was a boy. His brown hair remained as thick and lustrous as ever, although it was a little too long to be fashionable these days. His clothes were several years out of date, too, but reasonable enough, and more importantly his manner was as normal as ever it was.

A short time later, when the house steward announced dinner, they adjourned to the large dining room, which had, many years earlier, been built to replace the drafty great hall. The young visitor was surprised to see the table set with the magnificent Avedon silver-gilt service, glinting in the candlelight.

"I'm so relieved to find so many of the Avedon possessions still here," Hal ventured as they sat down at one end of the banqueting table.

"A good many objects from the Piccadilly house had to be sold, but I managed to retain much of what we have here."

Once they were seated, a game soup was served and the duke asked, "How is your mother nowadays, Hal?"

"She is in rude health, I thank you, Your Grace."

"These days life is informal here. Call me Oliver." Once again Hal's cheeks were tinged with pink. "And I am delighted to hear that your mother is well. You must convey my good wishes to her when you return home."

"She would be delighted to receive you, should you wish to visit her at Mapplewood."

"No doubt, but Summerhills keeps me exceedingly busy, and when I leave, it is to visit my other estates. Mayhap in the summer she will visit me here. Does she go about much nowadays?"

"Not a great deal. Occasionally she visits Aunt Sybil at Chepstow, but since Papa died, she seems not to enjoy going abroad as much as she did."

"That is a great pity for a handsome woman still young."

"I promise you, she does enjoy a diverse social life in and around Middlehampton. We have many friends."

The footmen removed their plates, and various dishes were brought in and placed on the table. The two diners helped themselves to a selection of fowl, fish, and meat, together with various dishes of vegetables.

"Your table is superb, Oliver."

"Everything is bred, grown, or fished on the Summerhills estate," the duke told him, his pride reflected in his manner. "We even have a herd of deer to provide us with venison. I believe it is true to say, we are almost self-sufficient here."

"I am full of admiration for you," Hal told him as he forked food into his mouth with gusto. "I could learn a good deal from you."

"I shall certainly endeavor to show you all we've achieved at Summerhills, and hope it will be useful to you at Mapplewood."

"There is one thing I have always wanted to ask. . . ." When the duke looked at him curiously, he swallowed. "Papa once told me that the Avedon fortune was founded on piracy. Is that really true?"

The duke smiled and reached for his glass of wine. "Privateering, to be more accurate. The first duke did sterling duty to Queen Elizabeth as a privateer, but he also contrived to enrich himself at the same time. When he was enobled by Her Majesty, he built this house and became respectable at last—or so I am given to believe."

The young man laughed. "How famous! I wish I had less mundane blood in my veins. I am descended from farmers to a man!"

His host leaned forward to refill his glass. "Let me tell you, Hal, you have the blood of a most splendid man in your veins, and that of your dear mother, too."

"I know it, you may be sure." After a moment Hal ventured, "In any event you were not obliged to resort to privateering to restore your family fortune."

"Just several years of hard work, speaking of which, I understand you are succeeding admirably managing your own estate. Don't think I don't interest myself in such matters."

"Partridge, Papa's land steward is still with us, and he is an excellent man, as you no doubt recall, and Mapplewood is only a fraction of the size of your landholdings."

"Nevertheless, your success so far augurs well for the future."

"You are very kind to say so."

"It is only the truth."

As the servants removed their plates and all the dishes, the young man said, "I am much more of a countryman than my father was."

The duke laughed as various pies and puddings were placed before them. "How true! Perry was never more happy than when he was in London or Brighton with Prinny. If only you knew of some of the larks we used to cut up."

"I recall he did tell me of one or two!"

"It's as well you don't know the whole of it." As Hal was served with some plum duff, the duke refused any of the puddings, and instead reached out to take an orange from a silver-gilt epergne. "Do you ever go up to London, Hal?"

"Occasionally—to see my tailor mostly—and I confess it is diverting, but I prefer to be at home at Mapplewood, and I am always glad to return. That is where I am happiest."

His guardian smiled at him across the table. "I understand that very well, although it took me a good deal longer than you to discover the fact."

After Hal had eaten his fill, the table was cleared and the cover removed. When the house steward brought out the port and glasses, the duke announced that they would take it in the drawing room.

"As you wish, Your Grace," the house steward replied impassively.

"I have often wondered if you miss the beau monde," Hal ventured as he savored the excellent port when they were once again seated in the drawing room. "You were one of its leading beaux only a few years ago."

"When I was your age, I never came to the country. My time was spent, like your father's, between London and Brighton, or visiting Newmarket and attending house parties. Then when my father died, I discovered he hadn't paid any attention to estate business to the great detriment of our finances. By enjoying ourselves so thoroughly, we'd all, including my brother John, beggared our fortune." He glanced around the beautiful room, filled with elegant and valuable furniture and paintings. "I almost lost all this."

He got up to refill their glasses, having dismissed the servants. "As I said, Oliver, you've succeeded so well. Summerhills is probably more prosperous now than it ever has been before."

"There is no doubt about that," the duke replied as he sat down again, "and I can tell you it is a most satisfactory sensation."

Mr. Turlington sipped at his port thoughtfully before he ventured, "I can easily appreciate the reason you were obliged to spend so much time here—several years in fact—but surely you are long past the time when you were unable to leave Summerhills. You could easily return to London during the social Season."

"My dear boy, I have absolutely no wish to do so. It is a great relief, I promise you, not to be obliged to consider what color coat to wear each morning or spread my favors with scrupulous equality between various females, so that it won't be assumed I am about to offer for one of them! Being considered a catch can be tedious in the extreme. Just wait until you join the ranks of those in search of a wife, and you will see what I mean."

Once again, the young man looked uncomfortable. "When I was a child, you were always the best companion a boy could have. You used to take me fishing and shooting, and I always thought you would make a splendid father to your own children."

"Once, perhaps, that might have been possible, but I was obliged to attend my financial affairs, which took all my energies for so long. Summerhills is too demanding a mistress to allow me time for a wife."

"What of an heir, though, if you do not consider me impertinent for mentioning it?"

"My brother, Lord John Barrington, is my heir. He's a buffoon, but I am resigned to knowing it is he or one of his children who will succeed me."

"I don't believe I am acquainted with his lordship, am I?"

"Probably not," the duke answered heavily as he drained his glass.

"Is . . . is he a black sheep?" the young man asked hesitantly.

His guardian laughed softly. "By no means. When we discovered ourselves newly impoverished, my brother immediately set about seeking an heiress to marry. He succeeded beyond his wildest expectations. My sister-in-law is not only the daughter of a city merchant, but is also compliant and adoring of a man who, like many others, is less than perfect." After a moment's hesitation, His Grace added thoughtfully, "I am obliged to you for your interest in my life, Hal, but what of you? How long do you intend to remain at Summerhills? We could go fishing tomorrow, or shooting if you prefer. And I am longing to show you over the entire estate."

Yet again the young man looked disconcerted. "I must return home on the morrow, Oliver, much as I would wish to stay and go out on the estate with you."

The duke frowned. "This is evidently a very short stay."

11

"I only wish it could be longer. Mayhap on another occasion, when I don't catch you unprepared for me."

"You are very welcome to stay," the duke reiterated.

Once again, the young man displayed a certain embarrassment. "If only it were possible. . . ."

"Hal, why did you really come? I have had the feeling all evening there is more to your visit than you have yet owned."

Mr. Turlington swallowed noisily. "You have been the most generous of guardians, Oliver. You have always been understanding of my wishes and needs. Your guardianship has some time to go until I am of an age when I may, under the terms of Papa's will, take charge of my own affairs. . . ."

"Oh, cut line, Hal. Are you strapped for funds? Do you need a larger allowance now you are down from Oxford?"

The young man laughed and held up his hand. "Indeed not. As I told you earlier, I am always in funds. My needs in general are modest compared to my means."

"You are to be congratulated," the duke answered dryly, and then he became serious again. "What exactly is your difficulty?"

"I am in love and wish to solicit your approval of our marriage."

The duke stared at him in astonishment. "My stars! I'd never have guessed such a thing. You are a trifle young to be thinking of matrimony, Hal."

"Age is immaterial when one is in love."

Fighting his inclination to laugh in the face of such a sanctimonious statement coming from one so young, the duke asked in as reasonable manner as he could contrive, "Tell me all about her and how you met. I suppose she is a debutante."

"No." Hal looked disconcerted. "Miss Penrose, for that is her name, and I have known each other all our lives. We have been aware for many years that one day we would wish to marry. There has never been anyone else for either of us, and there never will."

"Remarkable," commented the duke with one finger pressed pensively to his lips. "How old is Miss Penrose?"

"Seventeen," Mr. Turlington replied, exhibiting some difficulty once more.

The duke drew in a sharp breath. "She is a mere child. At so tender an age, I don't suppose she will have yet had a come out."

"No, she has not. She would in other circumstances make her debut next Season, but as she has no wish to be on the catch for a husband, there is no point in her doing so. We may as well be married now as later."

"Are her parents in favor of the match?"

The young man shifted uncomfortably in the chair. "Mr. Penrose is willing to sanction our betrothal if you give your consent, but not otherwise. He is not willing to allow her to be betrothed to me for the necessary length of time until we are able to marry, should you refuse us permission."

"I see," breathed the duke. "And if I do not give my consent, what will then ensue?"

Hal's cheeks grew red. "She will be obliged to go up to London to make her debut."

"That is usually the desire of most young ladies."

"Miss Penrose wishes only to marry me. She informs me that to be obliged to have a Season will be exceedingly horrid to her."

"For one so young, she is remarkably firm-minded."

"We both are in this matter. However, I'm persuaded you can have no cause to deny us your blessing, Oliver. Miss Penrose is as sweet-natured as she is beautiful, and if such matters weigh with you—and I am sure they do not—she has an ample portion. I can assure you, there is no finer female in the entire world!"

"I have no reason to doubt the veracity of that statement, Hal, but I really do consider you both a little young for matrimony—at least as quickly as you propose. I advise you to give yourself—and Miss Penrose—a little more time."

The young man sat forward in his chair. "I have already told you, we have known each other most of our lives, much longer than most couples who meet during a London Season."

"No doubt, but neither of you have mixed freely with other young people."

Hal's lips became compressed into a stubborn line. "We have no need to."

"Forgive me, Hal, but I believe you do. You would be even more certain of your choice after a little social intercourse."

"We are already certain."

Striving to contain his mounting irritation, the duke insisted, "That might be true of you, but you cannot speak for some totty-headed chit just out of the schoolroom."

Mr. Turlington jumped to his feet. "I must protest, sir! I cannot allow you to malign my future wife in this manner!"

The duke raised one hand to forestall his ward's

anger. "I beg your pardon, Hal. I did not mean to imply any ill to Miss Penrose, who I am certain is a diamond of the first water." The young man became calmer, and his guardian went on, "I am merely able to view the matter with more impartiality than you. In my opinion, Miss Penrose has had little access to the company of other gentlemen, and although I do not doubt her devotion to you, I ask you, is it fair to tie her to marriage at such a tender age? Every female is deserving of a Season."

"There is no possible point!" his ward insisted. "She wants to marry me, and it is useless for her to waste several months engaging in pursuits in which she has no interest."

"That is a nonsense, Hal, and you know it. If she is truly in earnest, she will remain constant in her devotion to you."

The young man stood stiffly with his hands clenched at his sides. "Am I to understand you deny me permission to marry Miss Penrose?"

"I am merely postponing it, Hal," and then the duke added, with a conciliatory smile, "until the end of my guardianship."

"That is outside of enough! I don't want to wait so long. What would be the use?"

"You will both be that much older. I advise you to spend some time in London yourself, mixing socially while Miss Penrose does the same thing. If you are then both of the same mind . . ."

"If! I am bound to say, I consider you totally unreasonable."

"I believe I am being entirely reasonable. I would be failing in my duty as your guardian if I did not insist upon a period of reflection for you both."

"How kind of you!" Hal fumed. "You have not taken your duties as my guardian at all seriously in recent years, so you will be obliged to excuse me if I find this sudden interest in my affairs a trifle hypocritical!"

The duke got to his feet and put a muscular arm around his ward's trembling shoulders. "I mean it for the best, I assure you. Believe me, Hal, I know what I am about. You are very young and inexperienced, and Miss Penrose younger still."

"How can you know what you are about, Oliver?" the young man asked, his voice choked with suppressed anger. "You know the neither of us. You haven't clapped eyes upon me for years, and Miss Penrose never. Indeed, I am moved to say I find you sadly changed from the splendid man of my memory."

The duke drew back, frowning. "I beg of you, do not take me in dislike over this, Hal. Love was never lost for waiting."

His ward turned a pair of cold blue eyes on the duke then. "How could you possibly know? Has any woman ever truly loved you?"

The duke's jaw jutted proudly, and his dark eyes glittered with anger. "You presume too much, you young puppy!"

Hal stepped back a few paces and bowed his head a little. "I beg your pardon most humbly, Your Grace. What I said was unforgivable."

The duke waved a dismissive hand in the air. "It's forgotten, Hal. You're on your high ropes, and I fully understand why."

"If you do, you will reconsider your decision." He began to move back toward the door. "Thank you for your indulgence and time. I will impose upon you no longer." When he reached the door, he added, "I shall be leaving for Mapplewood as soon as practicable in the morning."

"Can you not stay a while longer so we can become reacquainted with one another?"

His ward's smile was a stiff one. "If I do, is there a chance you will change your mind?"

"I believe I am being perfectly reasonable in asking you to delay until you are legally entitled to manage your own affairs. It is not, after all, a lifetime."

"Then I think I won't stay any longer, Your Grace. Miss Penrose is anxiously awaiting the news I bring her, although I do not relish witnessing her disappointment."

"If she is as sensible a female as you lead me to believe, she will fully understand my reservations, and I do look forward to making her acquaintance eventually."

"You will be obliged to travel to London to do so, for she will be forced to undertake a Season if we do not become betrothed beforehand. As there seems little more for us to discuss, I shall bid you good night."

When he had gone, the room seemed suddenly empty and very quiet, save for the crackling of the logs on the fire. The duke unconsciously clenched his hand into a fist and turned to rest it on the mantel.

Staring into the leaping flames of the fire, oblivious to the discomfort of the heat, he was aware he had handled the matter badly, but he didn't doubt for one moment he had acted correctly. Many years earlier, he had given his dear friend, Perry Turlington, his word to care for his son with as much

17

diligence as he himself would have done. Therefore, he could not possibly give his permission for the couple to marry without a good deal of further thought and consideration, otherwise he would be failing in his duty.

Besides, he decided, this Miss Penrose could not possibly be the paragon Hal made her appear to be. In His Grace's considered opinion, no woman could be so perfect.

TWO

When a smart green and gold-painted curricle drew up outside the Clarges Street house of Lord and Lady Dunwoody, several heads turned to stare, at first in admiration of the splendid vehicle and then to identify the elegant driver, clad in a driving coat with so many capes, it was difficult to count them in one glance.

The driver handed the ribbons to his tiger, climbed down nimbly, and then marched up the steps. Lord Dunwoody's house steward took the visitor's hat and gloves before helping him off with his greatcoat.

"May I take the liberty of saying, Your Grace, what a pleasure it is to see you again?"

The duke tugged self-consciously at his new buff-colored coat and replied, "How kind of you to say so, Jenks. Is my sister at home?"

"Almost the entire family is, Your Grace," the house steward answered wryly.

"Dame Fortune must be smiling on me."

As the duke spoke, a young man came strolling down the stairs. When he saw the duke, he stopped and cried, "By all that blue! Uncle Oliver!"

The duke turned on his heel and demanded to

know. "Do you learn that kind of language at Eton nowadays, Adolphus?"

The young man was unabashed, even mischievous. "In the stables like everyone else, and I am Octavious."

The duke's face relaxed into a smile. "I shall never be able to tell, even though you have grown apace since I last saw you."

"Mama always laments that we outgrow our clothes quicker than she can buy them, but at least she is able to pass them down to our brothers."

"I am persuaded she does nothing of the kind. Such economies are beyond your mother."

"Uncle Oliver!" Another voice caused the duke's head to snap upward to see Octavious's twin coming down the stairs.

"You are still so alike," the duke marveled. "How are you two boys faring at Eton?"

"Splendidly," they chorused.

Just then Lord Dunwoody came out of his study and cried, "Avedon! How good it is to see you after all this time!"

After much handshaking and slapping of backs, Greville Dunwoody said, "We're so glad you're back in town, and looking so prime, too."

The duke appeared to be somewhat abashed. "I have taken pains to replenish my wardrobe, which is not before time, so you need not say so."

"Wouldn't dream of it, old boy," his brother-in-law assured him.

"I was, in fact, most impressed by the new Burlington Arcade, which has sprung up since I was last in town."

"London is like a giant building site these days,"

the earl replied, sounding disgusted. "Prinny has some grand plan he's putting into motion."

"I was only just saying that the boys continue to be identical, Greville."

The earl looked surprised. "Do you really think so? It's easy for me to tell them apart."

The duke laughed. "Of course it is! You're their father, but I assure you it is almost impossible for others."

Lord Dunwoody stroked his chin thoughtfully. "Really? That is most interesting." He started suddenly as he espied through the window the duke's new carriage. "Good grief! Is that your curricle, Avedon?"

His brother-in-law could not hide his tone of satisfaction as he replied, "It was delivered from Hatchet's only this morning."

"And drawn by four bloods, rather than the usual two." Octavious pointed out.

"They'll get up to tremendous speed," his twin gasped.

"The cattle look like rum prancers," Lord Dunwoody murmured.

"They are prime bloods, all of them, the wheelers are particularly fine, but judge them for yourself, Grev."

"You may be certain that I will."

"So will we," his sons avowed.

"Will you allow me to tool the ribbons, Uncle Oliver?" Octavious asked.

"Perhaps," his uncle replied teasingly.

"If you do," Adolphus intercepted, "you will be obliged to allow me also."

"Naturally."

Lord Dunwoody transferred his attention to his

brother-in-law once again. "I could not be more pleased to see you so prime, Avedon. After the mess your late father left behind, we were persuaded the heart had gone out of you."

The duke smiled faintly as he watched his nephews, still attempting to discover some difference in their appearance. "Quite the contrary, I assure you."

Lord Dunwoody glanced quickly at his pocket watch. "Go along, boys, and fetch your coats and hats," he instructed as he put the watch away. "We shall be leaving presently."

"You're not going back to Summerhills yet, are you, Uncle Oliver?" Adolphus asked.

"Do say you're staying," urged his brother.

The duke smiled. "I intend to remain in town for a while, but in any event, I vow I shall not return to Summerhills without allowing you each to tool the ribbons."

"We always consider you bang up to the mark," Octavious told him.

"Top of the trees," his brother added.

Chattering excitedly, the twins ran up the stairs, leaving their uncle chuckling in the hall. "Oh, for the enthusiasm of youth!"

"They've always admired you, Oliver."

"There must be better role models, I fancy, but there is no doubt they are fine boys, Grev."

"I own, I am most fortunate in my family, due mainly, I am bound to confess, to their excellent mother. I am taking the boys with me to Cribb's Parlor. There will be many of your old acquaintances there, and I know they're all longing to see you again, including those with whom you used to spar so well. Do say you'll come with us."

"Much as I would like that, Grev, I have come today on a long, overdue visit to my sister. She will never forgive me if I go out without paying my respects."

"On another occasion, I will insist that you accompany us."

"On another occasion, I assure you there will be no need."

The earl hesitated for a moment before he put an arm around his brother-in-law's shoulders and drew him to one side. "Avedon," he said softly, "there has been some controversy abroad as to the reason for your return to town after so long a time. . . ."

The duke's eyes sparkled with amusement. "I can imagine what is being said, but if the tattle was not about me, it would be about some other poor fellow."

"One of the more popular notions, and one which your sisters hope is true, is that you have returned to society in order to seek a bride."

The duke laughed out loud. "That is absolutely out of the question, Grev."

"Valeria and Meribel will be grievously disappointed to hear that."

"They will have to endure their disappointment stoically, for I have no intention of putting myself in the parson's mousetrap simply to oblige them!"

"Well said, Avedon!" the earl applauded. "Don't be petticoat led, not that you ever were!"

At that moment the twins returned, and a few minutes later the duke was ushered into his sister's private drawing room. As the footman closed the door behind him, the duke was somewhat taken aback by the scene he encountered, and even more by the noise. His sister, Valeria, was sitting on a sofa, surrounded by children, all of whom were making a good deal of commotion.

When Lady Dunwoody became aware of her brother's presence, she squealed, "Oliver, my dear! How splendid to see you back in town. A visit is long overdue."

The clutch of children who had been milling around her turned their attention on the newcomer. "Uncle Oliver!" some of them chorused, fussing around him. One small tot even had the temerity to pull at his new coat.

"Children!" Lady Dunwoody called, and they quieted a little, much to the duke's relief.

"Valeria, are all these yours?"

"Of course they are. Don't you remember?" She pointed to each one in turn. "Magnus, Penelope, Philip, John, Mary, and, of course, Cleo."

The duke turned to the last-named child, a fast-growing young lady of latent beauty whose cheeks were pink and eyes bright.

"How you've grown, Cleo. You were a child when I last saw you. Now you are grown up and most pleasing, I own."

The girl adopted a modest attitude by lowering her eyes. "Thank you kindly, Uncle Oliver."

"The temptress of the Nile. How aptly you are named."

The girl's cheeks grew even more pink, and she bit her lip to suppress a smile while Lady Dunwoody chortled loudly.

"Such a tongue-pad, Oliver. How relieved I am to hear you in such good form."

"Am I not correct?" he asked, looking somewhat mystified.

"My eldest daughter was named for our Aunt

Fosbury, as you are well aware. Off you go, children. You will have other opportunities to see your uncle while he is in town."

Obediently Cleo shepherded the younger children out of the room, pausing by the door to cast her uncle a shy smile.

"In a very few years, she will be setting male hearts aflutter, Valeria," he told her as he came farther into the room.

Lady Dunwoody's eyes rolled heavenward. "Don't I know it! And if some of the gentlemen are like you . . ."

The duke raised her hand to his lips. "Why, Valeria, how can you say so? Surely you know I live an exemplary life."

"You haven't always," she teased. "How I recall some of your exploits! You and John. People still talk of them even now."

As he sat down in a high-backed chair close to her, he asked, "Wasn't there another child called Arthur? Or am I becoming justifiably confused?"

"Little Arthur is still in the nursery. If you wish to see him, I suggest you visit him there before you leave us."

Her brother held up one hand in mock surrender. "No, I thank you. I believe I shall wait until he is old enough to ride, or at least until he is out of leading strings. *You* appear to be in rude health, in any event. I wonder if you have any news for me."

She chuckled. "Indeed, I do not! This is one Season, I am determined not to be in an interesting condition or nursing an infant. Have you seen Grev as yet?"

"I encountered him downstairs when I arrived, and the boys, too."

"Ah yes, the twins. James is at Eton. Octavious and Adolphus should be there with him, too, but they are recovering from a particularly nasty bout of influenza. Oliver you have no notion how worrying it is to have so many children."

"You would concern yourself more if you had only the one."

Lady Dunwoody looked pensive for a moment before she replied, "Yes, I daresay you are correct. Have you seen Meribel yet?"

The duke looked wry. "I did call around to see her, but was relieved to find her out. I need a little more time to pluck up my courage to visit my eldest sister."

"And John?"

"I haven't seen him yet."

"Poor Betsey has redecorated their house, and it is quite hideous. She is as ever a cod's head. You can imagine, can you not, how easily Meribel casts her into the sullens?"

Her brother laughed. "Indeed, I can! No doubt John contrives to do that, too."

"Our brother continues to behave as he always has, with no consideration for anyone except himself. He makes no attempt to hide his liaisons from poor Betsey, who says not a word."

"You know full well she is more than content to be titled Lady Elizabeth Barrington. Nothing else is of any consequence to her."

"Perhaps not to her father, Mr. City Mushroom himself. I am not so certain poor Betsey is so happy. She always looks like a dying crab in a thunderstorm!"

Once again her brother laughed, and Lady Dunwoody went on, "Enough about them. What of you,

Oliver? You have come back to London, and I couldn't be more delighted. You look slap up to the nines again, which is not before time, I assure you. The last time I visited you at Summerhills, you looked decidedly shabby."

"Never!" the duke exclaimed, looking shocked.

"It's true, but I knew it was a temporary aberration, and I can see that all is mended, although I should not venture to say that it is positively *fashionable* to be absent from London nowadays."

"Who has decreed that, Valeria?"

"His Majesty is at Windsor . . ."

"He is totally mad."

"Brummell has fled to Calais to escape his creditors."

"So I heard, but truly, my dear, I don't believe on this occasion he will start a fashion."

"If not, it will be the first time, but seriously, Oliver, how is that for a gentleman to behave?"

"Papa always declared that Brummell was *not* a gentleman."

Valeria laughed. "Yes, I recall. And that fool, Byron, after bewitching everyone with his poetry, has gone to the Continent, abandoning his wife and child. I was never more shocked. It's said that he put his curls in papers at night. Women were his ruination, Oliver."

The duke began to laugh. "They usually are for most men."

"Fie to you!" she laughed. "He was in a case of pickles over Caro Lamb, you know. She is gone from London, too. It's said she is totally deranged. *I* thought she always was. With all these departures, the Season could be a dead bore, but now you are back. . . ."

Her brother continued to look amused. "If nothing else, Valeria, I shall be able to catch up on all the tattle while I'm here."

The countess looked rueful. "Ah, as for tattle, Oliver dear, there is a good deal concerning *you* just now."

"It is good to learn that very little changes."

"There are two conflicting *on-dits* concerning you, my dear, that have been around for years."

His dark brown eyes opened wide with surprise. "I am, indeed, honored. Two *on-dits*."

"Less popular is the rumor that when you returned to Summerhills, you were unable to repair the family fortune, and so you are obliged to live your life in poverty and loneliness."

"No doubt clad in tatters," the duke commented as he took a pinch of snuff. "No wonder Ridgeway offered me a loan when I encountered him in Pall Mall this morning. It was puzzling at the time, but abundantly clear after what you have just disclosed."

Lady Dunwoody attempted to stifle her laughter with the palm of her hand pressed to her lips. "Oh, how famous! You're as rich as the Golden Ball! How could he be such a lobcock?"

"After your last disclosure, I cannot wait to hear what the most popular *on-dit* says of me. I daresay, like most *on-dits,* it is a masterpiece of invention."

His sister's eyes twinkled merrily. "We may jest about it, Oliver, but to Meribel and I, it is often most vexatious."

"I am certain you contrive handsomely."

"However much we deny such rumors, naturally we are not entirely believed."

"What you and Meribel say is not relevant, my dear."

"No, indeed," she replied, composing herself once more. "There are certain sections of the ton who truly believe your recent and prolonged seclusion is due to your . . ."

"My what, Valeria?" he asked politely.

". . . your lunacy." After looking astonished for a moment or two, his laughter rang out, much to his sister's relief. "I have myself heard it said that you are guarded by trusted servants day and night in a locked room at Summerhills."

The duke was still laughing as he replied, "I do believe I prefer *that* high-flyer to the other one. It is much more colorful."

"It certainly is the easier to disprove now you are back in town."

"I am not so sure. I shall be obliged to go very carefully indeed, lest my mental condition is blamed for any eccentric act I may perform."

"Our brother, John, does not do much to discourage such talk, I fear. He always says to anyone who inquires of you, using an ingratiating smile that certain females find irresistible, that you were always a little *different*."

"And here was I foolishly imagining he would be welcoming me back to the ton."

"Since you've been ruralizing, my dear, our brother has become a leader of fashion."

"No doubt, but why should my return vex him so?"

"Because you were always all the crack. Dear Johnny wouldn't wish you to replace him in the forefront of fashionable circles."

"He has nothing to fear from me."

Lady Dunwoody looked all at once serious. "Oliver, why *have* you come to town just now?"

He shifted uncomfortably in the chair. "Before I tell you, I must first ask for your complete discretion. What I have to say is for you only to know."

"You have my word," she replied, looking intrigued.

"Not even Meribel."

The countess smiled. "Especially not Meribel."

"I received a visit from my ward, Henry Turlington a few weeks ago . . ."

Lady Dunwoody sighed. "That tiresome boy."

"Hal is not in the least tiresome."

"Willful and spoiled then. He has been woefully spoiled, you know. You might not be aware of it, but Caroline has indulged him shamefully, especially after Perry died."

"That is not so surprising."

"No, I daresay there is some truth in that, but what is his problem? Is he in the suds?"

"No, he is in love."

Lady Dunwoody laughed merrily before saying, "Hurrah for callow youths!"

"The problem is, he wants to be married as soon as possible."

"He's so young!"

"A fact I tried to point out to him, but he appears quite set upon this course, despite all my advice to the contrary. In fact, I am sorry to say, we parted brass rags."

"Oh dear, how unpleasant for you. One should never attempt to thwart spoiled brats, Oliver."

The duke frowned. "At least he hasn't grown up rakish or dissipated, or indeed wishing to become leg-shackled to some opera dancer."

"Well, you're evidently not enthusiastic about the match. Is the young lady a fortune hunter?"

The duke shrugged his broad shoulders. "That's the fix, Valeria. I have no notion. Hal tells me she is a beauty and an heiress to boot, which makes my opposition to an immediate marriage seem rather foolish, only I cannot in all conscience sanction the match without giving it a good deal more consideration than he required of me."

"He must have told you something about her."

"All I know is that her name is Penrose, and she lives in Middlehampton with her family."

Valeria Dunwoody frowned. "Penrose? Can it be Araminta Penrose? Oh, surely not."

Again he shrugged. "Do you actually know a family by that name from the Middlehampton area?"

"Indeed I do."

"So you must know the chit Hal fancies himself in love with!"

"If it is Araminta Penrose, and I'm persuaded it couldn't be anyone else. Oh, Oliver dearest, you have no cause to concern yourself! Mr. Turlington displays all good sense, for Minty is a fine girl. I have been acquainted with Bella, her mother, since we were girls."

The duke looked both surprised and pleased. "This is a piece of good fortune I had not expected, Valeria. You can confirm that this chit is all Hal has said she is."

"I would have considered Minty Penrose a little too full of good sense to fall in love with Hal Turlington."

When Lady Dunwoody began to look troubled,

her brother prompted, "You'd better tell me everything."

"There is nothing to tell, except ... well, I am bound in all honesty to tell you, she is certainly *not* a beauty in any of the accepted senses, as you are bound to discover for yourself, and although the Penrose family has excellent connections—Bella, too—they are not in the least wealthy. I know that dear little Minty is not possessed of a fortune, and that is why I am doing all I can to take her up during her Season. I had not thought her chances of contracting a good marriage at all favorable, but if she has caught the fancy of Hal Turlington ..."

She cast her brother a doubtful look as he said in clipped tones, "So the little minx has misrepresented herself, has she not?"

"Oh, I don't believe that is so for one moment! More likely Mr. Turlington has mistaken the matter of their wealth, for they contrive to live comfortably enough, I fancy, and beauty is different to individuals, don't you think?" she ended in a hopeful tone.

"No," the duke replied.

Lady Dunwoody smiled uncomfortably. "I do recall in your salad days, you always had an accredited beauty in your carriage, but if everyone was of a like mind, there would be little hope for the rest of us."

"There is an element of truth in what you say, Valeria, but I really cannot see how Hal could possibly mistake her financial situation. He has lived in close proximity to the family for most of his life, as far as I am aware. He may be a little naive, but he is no ninnyhammer. It seems to me, Miss Penrose might be rather more clever than he."

"It is possible . . ."

"I have come to town to investigate the matter, and it appears now it is imperative that I do so with no further delay."

"Do not, I beg of you, get on your high ropes, for I am persuaded there has been some misunderstanding that can easily be explained. The Penroses are the nicest people—not at all *tonnish*, if you know what I mean."

The duke appeared not to be listening, and he said darkly, "I shall look into the matter personally. Any attempt to bubble my ward will not escape me."

"Oliver . . ." his sister began, and then she uttered a sigh, falling into silence.

"How can I best make her acquaintance?" he asked.

"They have rented a house for the Season in Berkeley Street. Why don't you call in and present yourself?"

"I am not so insensitive, my dear. I would prefer to make an initial appraisal of Miss Penrose in more informal circumstances, if at all possible. I do assume they go out in society."

"They are attending a rout party I am giving here next Thursday evening," Lady Dunwoody informed him in a muted tone.

"That is most convenient," he allowed.

"I felt it incumbent upon me to assist Bella as much as possible, as they have not gone out in society overmuch and would not normally mix in the highest circles."

Just as the duke was about to stand up, his sister said, "I am grievously disappointed in you, Oliver."

Arrested, he responded, "You will, no doubt, inform me how I have contrived to commit this outrage against you, Valeria."

"I had hoped—Meribel and I, in fact, hoped—that you had come to seek a bride for yourself and end your dreadful solitude."

He laughed at the very notion. "No, I thank you. I am a confirmed bachelor. I happen to like my life the way that it is. My solitude is not in the least dreadful."

"Pamela Westcot is going out in society again."

"Pamela Westcot?" he asked, looking genuinely puzzled.

"She was Pamela Harwell, you must recall."

"Ah!"

"You were once very fond of her."

"Yes, I recall."

"Charlie Westcot died last year. He was thrown from a horse while out hunting, and cracked his skull. He never regained his senses. Poor Pammy was inconsolable for a long while."

"Am I to take it, she is now willing to be consoled, Valeria?"

Lady Dunwoody cast him a disgusted look. "You are so cold, Oliver. You never used to be so cold."

"As I recall, Miss Harwell was very receptive to my attentions until she discovered my fortune was nonexistent. There is something cold about that, you must own, my dear."

"Well, in any event Westcot has left her rather rich. She has many suitors."

"I am so glad to hear it." She got to her feet, and he kissed her hand. "I must leave now, Valeria dearest. I have a fitting for my new evening coat."

"You really haven't changed, my love! How wonderful it is to see you acting just as you used to do."

The duke smiled sardonically. "You would not wish me to attend your rout dressed like a tatterdemalion. Think of all the tattle that would cause!"

She chuckled and laid her head on his shoulder as they walked toward the door. "It really is good to see you in town again, dearest, but I do beg of you not to judge Miss Penrose too harshly. I cannot help but feel the error must be on Mr. Turlington's part. In his anxiety to gain your approval, he has misrepresented her, but that is not her fault."

"We shall see what transpires."

"That is what troubles me, Oliver. Miss Penrose is unused to gentlemen of great consequence. She wouldn't know how to deal with a nonpareil."

"Good. That means I shall be able to knock her pretensions into horse nails with very little ado. I might have lived in some seclusion at Summerhills for the past few years, but I still know how best to win over bread-and-butter females. She might believe she has brought Hal up to scratch, but chits have always fallen like autumn leaves around me."

"Oliver!" Her eyes were wide, and he laughed even when she said, "You might well receive a shock."

More seriously the duke explained, "I don't like to see a young man like Hal petticoat led, and it is evident to me that is what is happening. He is still my ward, and I owe it to his dead father to ensure he becomes a man before he hangs up his ladle, but you can rely upon me to be scrupulously fair in my dealings with Miss Penrose. I really do hope she is the perfect female for my ward."

Just as she cast him a doubtful glance, they came to the head of the stairs and espied their elder sister, Meribel Stanyon, coming into the hall. As she paused to strip off her gloves in a purposeful manner that was typical of her, the duke groaned inwardly and Lady Dunwoody became alert.

When Lady Stanyon caught sight of them, a look of annoyance crossed her face. "Avedon, I would have thought that as I am your elder sister by some years, it would have been more appropriate for you to call upon me first."

The duke cast a wry glance at Lady Dunwoody, and then hurried down the stairs to greet his other sister. Disregarding her ferocious stare, he raised both her hands to his lips.

"I could not agree with you more, Meribel. I did call upon you first, you may be sure, but you were not at home."

The marchioness's annoyance faded. "My mistake, Oliver, for I know I can rely upon you not to disregard form. You can have no notion how lax standards have become of late. Why . . ."

"We shall have the lengthiest of cozes as soon as is possible," he promised, cutting off the impending diatribe. "Just now I leave you with Valeria. You evidently have much to say to her."

The woman smiled at last and said conspiratorially, so that only he could hear, "You have no notion how much advice on the upbringing of children our sister requires."

"She is most fortunate to have you to guide her in that most important of tasks."

"You'll be interested to know, I have been visiting Poor Betsey just now. Our sister-in-law is such a goosecap, but 'tis no wonder with a husband like John. She has just completed the redecoration of their house, and it transpires she has entirely disregarded all my good advice."

36

The duke's lips twitched slightly, but he appeared perfectly sober as he replied, "How foolish of her."

"Her attitude in this matter has wounded me, naturally, but worse, she has no taste. None at all. That much is evident by her choice of husband. Now, I can see you wish to be gone about your business, so I shall not detain you any longer. But I will call upon you very soon, I promise. I am in a fidge to see the house. It has been closed for so long."

When she started up the stairs, the duke cast a sympathetic smile to Lady Dunwoody and then, retrieving his outdoor clothes, went to his new curricle. As he drove away, his thoughts returned to Araminta Penrose and his self-appointed task of ascertaining whether she was a scheming vixen or truly as enamored of Hal as he was of her.

In truth, he was not at all relieved by what Valeria had to tell him. He knew his sister well enough to appreciate she never said anything truly malicious about anyone, and if Mrs. Penrose was a friend, it was more like she would wish to see the daughter well settled. However, he had in his youth seen close at hand the efforts of scheming females to entrap wealthy young bachelors, and he was determined not to allow his ward to fall into the clutches of such a creature. It was, after all, his duty to prevent it.

THREE

"So here is where you're hiding, Minty," Miss Araminta Penrose's mother declared as she closed the door to the drawing room in their rented house.

The young lady, who had been sitting by the window, her nose buried in a book, started. "Oh, Mama, how you startled me!"

"I do beg your pardon, my dear," Bella Penrose replied, hurling herself into a chair. "How unlike you to be so easily overset."

Miss Penrose laughed. " 'Tis only this book that I borrowed from the circulating library yesterday. It is truly terrifying!"

Mrs. Penrose reached out to see the title. "What an odd title. *Frankenstein*. It sounds German to me."

"It is written by Mrs. Shelley, the wife of the poet. How talented they are, Mama."

"I daresay, but you should not be reading so much, Minty. Gentlemen don't like bookish females. You must exercise extreme care not to appear a bluestocking."

Again the girl laughed. "I don't give a fig for what gentlemen like or do not like. They all seem to like gaming, which in my opinion is a crack-brained thing to do, given the low ebb they find themselves in afterward."

Mrs. Penrose clucked her tongue. "You have not been remiss in enjoying the fruits of their foolishness."

"For chicken stakes only, Mama. Here in town, clubs exist, I am told, expressly for the purpose of gaming large amounts. Is that not how the last Duke of Avedon lost his fortune?"

"My dear child, now that we are in London, you must contrive to be less fulsome in your opinions. It is not appreciated."

"I cannot remain silent to please gentlemen, however toplofty they are. It is a great fault in me, I fear."

Her mother clucked her tongue once again. "You would have been better served coming out with me this morning than straining your eyes over that book. It only serves to fill your head with fanciful notions."

Unabashed, the girl asked, "Did you procure the lace you were seeking?"

"Yes, indeed, and there was a good deal of it at Layton and Shear. I also purchased some wonderful suede gloves, although I am ashamed to confess they were rather expensive for my purse."

"On this occasion, Mama, you need not trouble your head, for Uncle Hubert is paying the shot."

"That is no excuse for us to be free with his money, Minty," Mrs. Penrose retorted. "We have much reason to be grateful to your uncle. Without his generosity, we should not be here, and you would not be able to enjoy a Season."

Araminta looked about to say something, but she did not and a euphoric expression came upon her mother's face. "It really is so easy to shop here in London, although I am bound to declare it is totally exhausting."

Araminta smiled indulgently at her mother. "You really are enjoying yourself, aren't you, Mama?"

Mrs. Penrose's face took on a suddenly impish look. "I confess that I am. It is so long since I sojourned in London. I had quite forgotten how exciting it can be." She frowned anxiously in her daughter's direction. "You are enjoying yourself, are you not, my dear?"

"I confess to finding myself more diverted than I anticipated, but when my Season is over, I shall be glad enough to return to Middlehampton."

Mrs. Penrose drew a deep sigh. "I know how your heart and thoughts remain there, but there is so little to be done in that direction. . . ." All at once her face became animated once again, "I forgot to tell you, a letter from Fanny has arrived."

All at once Araminta was roused from her reverie. "Oh, do tell me what she says! Is she finally recovered from her indisposition?"

"It is much worse than a mere indisposition, I fear." Mrs. Penrose shook her head sadly. "Poor Fanny is quite ill, it seems. Hubert has a notion he will bring her to London when she is well enough to travel to consult His Majesty's physician."

A bubble of laughter escaped Araminta's lips. "Oh, Mama, what would be the use? The physician has not helped His Majesty one jot. He remains as mad as ever." At her mother's outraged expression, she added quickly, "Don't fret, Mama. I'm persuaded Fanny will soon be as right as a trivet."

"At least I am able to declare that not all the

news is bad. I encountered my dear friend Lady Dunwoody this morning. She informs me she is most impressed by you, my dear."

Araminta looked more than a little discomforted by the revelation, although she responded, "I am truly obliged to her for saying so."

"She has promised to try and obtain vouchers for Almack's for us. Isn't that kind of her?"

"Most kind," Araminta agreed, although she looked less than ecstatic.

"You could display a little more enthusiasm, dearest. Lady Dunwoody has the ear of Lady Jersey and Mrs. Drummond-Burrell!"

"Lady Dunwoody is the most condescending lady imaginable, Mama, and I confess to liking her exceedingly well, only . . . Well, I cannot help but recall that she is the sister of that odious man."

"Lord John Barrington? What has his lordship done to displease you?"

Araminta gave a gasp of exasperation. "You know full well I don't mean Lord John Barrington."

"The Duke of Avedon," Mrs. Penrose said dully.

"Lord John Barrington is a proper coxcomb, but he would not, I'm persuaded, behave in the cavalier fashion demonstrated by his brother."

"Lord John behaves exactly as suits him, and as far as the Duke of Avedon is concerned, I recall he was always quite, quite charming."

Her daughter looked shocked. "Mama!"

"Yes, dear, I know full well your grounds for holding him in dislike, which I grant you are perfectly valid. His Grace's behavior with regard to a certain romantic attachment does seem a trifle unfair . . ."

"It is downright wicked. He doesn't care a jot if

he destroys the happiness of two people who are desperately in love, but I daresay that is because the man is a certified lunatic."

It was Mrs. Penrose's turn to look shocked. "Minty! You must not say such a thing, even in the privacy of our own drawing room."

"Everyone says it, Mama. I am only repeating what has been told to me on countless occasions."

Mrs. Penrose shook her head. "If that dreadful *on-dit* held any vestige of truth, I'm persuaded Valeria Dunwoody would have confided it in me."

"She is not likely to confirm that her own brother is a lunatic, Mama, especially as Lord John is waiting for just such an opportunity to seize control of everything."

Her mother looked bewildered. "How do you know that, Minty?"

"Hal told me a long time ago. I have urged him to consult a solicitor to have the guardianship dissolved because of the duke's insanity."

"Is that possible?"

"I don't know, but if a king can be deprived of his powers because of his insanity, why not the Duke of Avedon?"

Mrs. Penrose shook her head. "You take too much upon yourself."

"I cannot sit back and do nothing, Mama, especially as I feel so wretched about it all."

"I understand that, but, recall, gentlemen do not like clever females, only decorative ones."

"I'm no more clever than I am decorative." Araminta frowned suddenly. "Something must be done and soon. It is utterly horrid to have one's life dictated to by a lunatic."

"Lunatic or not, Lady Dunwoody informs me that her brother has come at last to town."

The young lady looked shocked and was, unusually for her, stunned into silence for a few moments. At last she gasped, "After all this time?"

"Apparently so."

"Did Lady Dunwoody reveal to you his reason for leaving Summerhills just now? He has lived like a hermit there for years."

"No, she did not, and in all truth I would not expect it of her. I daresay, he has to attend to some business in town."

All at once, Araminta looked alarmed. "Oh, Mama, you do not think he has come in order to . . . inspect us?"

"Why should he?" Mrs. Penrose asked in bewilderment.

"Obviously because of our intended connection with his ward."

The woman shook her head. "No, no, Minty, he would not regard that of the least import. I am certain that is not his reason for coming to town at this time."

"I do hope you are correct, Mama, for I'm persuaded he will be sorely disappointed in us, and that would bode ill."

Mrs. Penrose sat up straight in her chair. "Araminta," she said, using her daughter's full name in a stern tone of voice, "should you encounter him at any time during his stay in London, I forbid you to say anything to him on the subject of Mr. Turlington and any possible nuptials."

"I shall not be able to stop myself, especially if it is he who speaks of it to me."

"In that event, if it is at all possible, do for once contrive to be less outspoken in your opinions."

"If I do encounter His Grace, he would consider it decidedly odd if I do not mention the matter to him."

"Even so, I entreat you to exhibit extreme caution."

"Do you think me a complete goosecap, Mama? Too much is at stake for me to risk alienating him further."

"You can be a trifle sharp when you choose. Your Aunt Basing considers it a great failing in you."

The girl looked vexed. "Do you think he might relent and give his permission for the marriage if I toadied to him?"

"I couldn't possibly say."

"You knew him, though."

"As a boy, a youth, and a young blade, yes, but not in recent years, and I remind you how the years wreak changes in all of us. He is said to be utterly changed."

She drew a sigh, and Araminta looked bright-eyed and suddenly eager. "You must tell me all about him, Mama. Everything you know. In a war, it is imperative to know as much about one's enemy as is possible."

"Minty! What a nonsensical attitude to this matter you have. War, indeed! Enemy!"

The girl thrust out her hands in a pleading manner. "This means so much to me. I must know what he is like. Hal veers between adoration and hatred in his attitude to his guardian."

Once again the woman sighed. "Oh dear, let me think. I know little enough in all conscience."

"Just think back and tell me all you remember."

Mrs. Penrose frowned with concentration. "When he came down from Oxford, he seemed rather wild, and that made him most attractive, but, I daresay, he was much like many others enjoying all the pursuits available to young gentlemen."

"Mr. Turlington is not in the least like that," Araminta said, looking pleased.

"That, I confess, is much in his favor. I just wish he was a little less serious."

"No one is ever perfect, Mama," her daughter answered sagely, "and I dislike intensely those gentlemen who style themselves Corinthians."

"Then you would have disliked His Grace in those days."

"Yes, I'm sure I should. Pray continue, Mama."

Mrs. Penrose smiled foolishly then. "He was devilishly handsome, as I recall. He had lovely dark eyes that were always full of humor and charm. He had more charm than a dozen others put together. However, everyone knew it would not do to anger him, for he possessed a foul temper. I once saw him out of patience with Lord John, and I was glad, I tell you, not to be standing in his shoes. However, I believe boredom was what suited him least. I have heard him put down many an old bore with a sharp word."

"He sounds formidable."

"I never considered him so, but then we were so very well acquainted. He had a devastating way of kissing a lady's hand."

"I had no notion there was a particular art in doing so," Araminta remarked, displaying some surprise.

"It was just that he turned the hand over and kissed the palm. It was a gesture that never failed to have its desired effect on any lady. I'm given to believe the beau monde was a good deal duller when he decided to ruralize."

Araminta smiled wryly. "Mama," she teased, "to hear you talk in such a manner makes me believe you were a little in love with him yourself."

Once again Mrs. Penrose smiled foolishly. "How can you say so? When His Grace came down from Oxford, I was already married to your dear Papa and a mother to boot."

"I won't gainsay the notion he might have been handsome and charming as well as devilishly attractive to totty-headed females—no disrespect to you, Mama—but as you so rightly said, the years have probably wrought a great change in him, and you must strive to remember he is now our enemy."

"Minty, I am fast losing patience with you. Our enemy, indeed! That is doing it too strong."

"Begging your pardon, Mama, but I do not think so. I only hope he has not been tempted out of his retreat in order to inspect us. That would be altogether too horrid of him."

"He is far too high in the instep to trouble his head over us. Once he refused Hal permission to marry, I fancy that would be the end of the matter to him. He would not condescend to think about it again."

Araminta gasped and looked shocked. "How can anyone be so unfeeling? He professes to be fond of Hal."

"You must not allow this situation, unfortunate as it is, to spoil your first Season, Minty. You cannot change anything by behaving downish."

"How can I behave in any other manner until this matter is resolved. My heart is so heavy. All the Season means to me now is an opportunity to visit the theaters, the concerts, and the museums, and," she added slyly, "St. Bartholomew's Fair."

Mrs. Penrose clucked her tongue. "I have already told you, that is out of the question for two ladies on their own." Then she went on to say, "If the matter teases you, I should tell you that I personally believe I know why the duke has come to town at this point." Her daughter looked at her with renewed interest. "When he was younger, he paid court to an accredited beauty, Miss Pamela Harwell. Beauty she had in abundance, but little fortune, rather like you, my dear . . ."

"I have no beauty either, Mama."

"Fustian, Minty. I do entreat you not to go about making such statements in public."

"It's true. Everyone will know it just by looking at me."

Mrs. Penrose strove to hide her irritation. "As I was saying, Pamela Harwell and the duke, or Lord Vayne, as he was known then, seemed assured of their future, until it transpired that the late duke had squandered most of his fortune and the incumbent was set to lose all, so she married Lord Westcot instead. The duke was said to be much affected."

Araminta clapped her hands together delightedly. "So that is the cause of his disobliging attitude! It really is so simple an explanation. Having been so ill-treated in love himself, he would not wish to enable others to enjoy connubial bliss!"

"I wish you would not read so many novels, Minty. I fear they are giving you fanciful notions. Pray, allow me to continue with what I was saying."

"I do beg your pardon, Mama," said her regretful daughter.

"Lady Westcot is now a widow and returning this Season to the social round. Lady Dunwoody told me all about her hopes for their eventual marriage. It is evident someone, probably one of his sisters, will have informed His Grace that Lady Westcot is about to return to town and is no doubt on the catch for a husband."

Araminta looked astounded. "Oh, surely he could not be such a nick-ninny to wear the willow for so long? From all I have heard of him, it seems most unlike that he has."

"As you know all too well, my dear, we must not underestimate the power of true love or its ability to endure."

Araminta drew a deep sigh at the reminder before she ventured, "Mayhap, if Lady Westcot is receptive to his advances this time. . . ."

"She will be. It is said he is richer now than ever he was, or Lord Westcot for that matter. It would be too much of a coincidence, I feel, if he was not returning to the social round because of her."

"Then perchance when he is, himself, contemplating a happy future, he will take pity on us and give his permission for the wedding!"

Mrs. Penrose smiled sadly. "I do hope so, for I know how much it will mean to you. But do not, I beg of you, depend upon it."

Araminta frowned in concentration. "Mama, do you recall if he possessed any weaknesses?"

Her mother looked rather perplexed. "No more than any other young man, unless you include a decided penchant for beautiful young ladies."

Once again, Araminta drew a profound sigh as

her mother got to her feet. "I do not know whether I wish to make his acquaintance or am excessively dreading doing so," she confessed.

As her mother moved quickly toward the door, she looked back and said, "It is no odds whatever you feel about it, Minty. You are bound to encounter him in the very near future."

FOUR

The rout party at Dunwoody House was in full progress when the Duke of Avedon arrived. Once the most inveterate of party goers, he now viewed the coming evening with a good deal of reluctance. The years spent in country pursuits—often rolling up his shirtsleeves to undertake much-needed manual work himself, where as once a speck of fluff on his superbly cut coat would have annoyed him, had dulled his appetite for such occasions.

Now he felt a little odd, clad in his new evening clothes. A black coat with silver buttons over a white waistcoat, pristine shirt, and white breeches were the ultimate in sartorial elegance—or so his tailor had assured him. So too was his new haircut, *à la Brutus*, replacing the unkempt style he had adopted in recent years. Elegant he might have looked, but the duke certainly felt more conspicuous than he liked.

As he surrendered his cloak to the lackey, he glanced around him in dismay, for the entire house seemed packed as tightly as possible with a seething mass of people. It had always been so on such occasions, he recalled, but he had become more accustomed to the many acres of Summerhills, a vast house with countless rooms that were available to him alone. The recollection that he used to relish such gatherings as this amazed him now as a crescendo of laughter and chattering assailed his ears, and a mixture of exotic perfumes reached his nostrils.

If he harbored any vague urge to withdraw, the emergence of his sister out of the crowd arrested his departure. "Your name is on everyone's lips this evening," she confided, "but shame on you for being so tardy. I secretly feared you might cry off."

"I almost did," he confessed, "but that would have nullified my reason for absenting myself from Summerhills, would it not?"

"Your reason?" she asked, looking perplexed.

"My ward's romantic affiliation," he explained, and her brow cleared immediately. "I can scarce call upon Miss Penrose and interview her as a prospective bride for my ward, can I?"

"It would not be beyond you," his sister chastised.

He took her hand at last and raised it to his lips. "I believe I haven't yet commented upon how ravishing you look tonight, my dear."

Looking nevertheless pleased, she replied, "Keep your flummery for those more receptive to it. However, you do look exceptionally handsome yourself tonight, Oliver."

Others were also admiring him, some wondering who he might be, while those who did know explained in some excitement to those who did not.

"Thank you, my dear," he responded. "I could not offend you by appearing in the clothes I am happy to wear at Summerhills."

"Style is something one never loses, Oliver. You will find the effort well worthwhile, for John and

Poor Betsey are here as well as Miss Penrose, not to mention Lady Westcot."

"No, do not mention Lady Westcot," the duke answered wryly.

"You will be kind to her, won't you, dear?"

"Valeria, when was I ever anything else?" he asked in outraged tones.

"She is most anxious to become reacquainted with you."

"She might be surrounded by so many admirers, she won't even notice my presence."

Lady Dunwoody laughed. "Do not depend upon that! John is quite convinced you are here to see Pammy, and because my lips are sealed on the matter of a certain young debutante, I cannot gainsay that notion with any credence."

"Then do not trouble yourself to do so. If our brother believes I may yet marry and—heaven forfend!—replace him as a leader of fashion, it will cause him no end of palpitations, and I have no intention of setting his mind at ease."

His sister laughed delightedly. "You are quite wicked, Oliver." She linked her arm into his. "Come, let us see who we can find. There are so many of your old acquaintances here tonight, and they're all in a fidge to see you again."

"Were rout parties always as crowded as this, Valeria?"

Again she laughed. "Some were—and still are—much worse than this."

"How on earth did I abide them?"

"As I recall, you always used to arrive early and were one of the last to leave. You usually staggered home as the sun came up."

The duke made a wry face. "Do not remind me of my rakehell days, my dear."

"I am bound to confess, I liked you a good deal better then."

He was somewhat taken aback by her pronouncement, but was given no opportunity to reply, as a large number of guests acknowledged him enthusiastically as he passed through the throng. They reached the ballroom, where added to the noise of conversation was the music of an orchestra on the balcony above the dance floor.

When he entered the ballroom, the duke paused to survey those already present. A good deal of attention was focused upon him, and he didn't doubt many were looking for signs of poverty, dissipation, and madness. For his part, he was searching the crowds for someone who might be Miss Penrose. He was now most anxious to make her acquaintance so that he could make an early departure. His attention came to rest upon one blushing beauty who averted her eyes and hid her bashfulness behind her fan.

Lady Dunwoody smiled and said, "Miss Faine, allow me to introduce His Grace, the Duke of Avedon."

Amid her great confusion, the duke engaged her for a dance later in the evening, but the moment he discovered she was not Araminta Penrose, his interest faded.

A few moments later, while the duke was being greeted on all sides, a gentleman emerged from the crowds. It was his brother, John, who despite gaining a little weight since they had last met appeared to be as good-looking as ever. Standing together, the brothers made a handsome pair, the duke a little taller than Lord John, but the younger brother a shade darker in coloring. At close quarters, the duke could see that his brother's habitual dissipation was beginning to take its toll upon his features, whereas the talk around the room was that the duke appeared as handsome as ever.

In their youth, the brothers had been known as Cupid and Apollo as they cut a swath through society and set many female hearts aflutter. Being penniless but well connected, John had married an heiress who had scarcely made any alteration to his romantic life-style.

Lord John Barrington greeted his brother affably. "This is good news if you've returned to the ton, Avedon. Good to see you."

"You look in great spout," the duke replied, displaying rather less enthusiasm in seeing his brother.

"As always, I assure you. Marriage is the answer. A man should have a wife. I'm persuaded you should step into the parson's pound."

Sensing his brother's anxiety behind the remark, the duke smiled affably. "Perhaps I will. I trust that your wife is quite well."

"Betsey has a stout constitution. There she is, in a fidge to see you," he indicated, leading the way. "Of course she is ever the wallflower."

Lady Elizabeth Barrington, known to the family as Poor Betsey, remained much as the duke recalled, plain, painfully shy, and dowdy, hugging the wall as if she needed it for support.

"Look who we have here," her husband cried, beaming with joviality. "What a splendid surprise, eh Betsey?"

Elizabeth Barrington smiled faintly, and the

duke, as always, felt desperately sorry for her. "Hello, Betsey," he said kindly, suspecting events such as these were an ordeal for her. "How are you?"

The woman murmured her response, and her husband continued in the same jovial tone of voice, "Betsey and I have had a discussion and decided we intend to hold a party in your honor, Avedon."

The duke held up one hand. "No need to trouble, none at all."

"Nonsense! You do intend to remain for the rest of the Season, don't you?"

"That all depends." The duke caught his sister's eye and added mischievously, "I am not certain how long my business in London will take."

Lord John looked intrigued. "Business, Avedon? What kind of business would that be, if you will pardon my asking?"

"It is of a personal nature, so you will have to excuse my discretion."

Lord John looked more than a little disgruntled, and suddenly his wife spoke out loud at last. "We would very much like to hold a party in your honor, Oliver, if it is agreeable to you."

Her husband looked as startled as the duke, who after a moment recovered himself to reply, "I couldn't possibly refuse such a charming invitation, my dear."

Predictably she blushed, and the duke was relieved when he was drawn away by an old friend.

"I couldn't believe m'own ears when I was told Oliver Avedon was back in town," Sir Leo Playfair remarked.

"It is good to see you, Leo."

Sir Leo lowered his voice. "I'm even happier to

know that ludicrous *on-dit* concerning your mental state will now be laid to rest."

"That will depend upon how I conduct myself while I'm here."

Sir Leo laughed heartily before he replied, "None of your old friends believed it, I assure you, only old tabbies gossiping over a dish of scandal broth could give credence to such tarradiddle."

"Well, we never paid much heed to them, did we, Leo?"

The two men continued to laugh, and then the duke asked, "Have you been caught in the parson's mousetrap yet?"

"No, indeed, and I don't intend to be, but it's rumored you have returned to fix your interest in a certain direction."

"If I don't, there are those who will definitely consider me a lunatic. I trust the tabbies will not be disappointed."

"Either way, someone will. A few of us are going down to Newmarket at the end of the week. Kingsbury has a filly running. Would you care to join us?"

"Delighted," the duke responded, and as he did so he caught sight of a young man leading his sister-in-law onto the dance floor. "Who's the cub sporting a toe with Lady Betsey?"

Sir Leo turned on his heel and raised his quizzing glass to his eye. "That's Sholto Farthington. Devilishly bad gamester. His pockets are always to let. He usually needs a *chère amie* to raise the wind for him. He recently parted brass rags with Emily Pellon."

The duke looked amused. "If he's intent upon fill-ing my sister-in-law's head with flummery, I don't give much for his chances of success."

"She's a female, ain't she? A pony says he'll succeed!"

"Done!" the duke responded with a laugh.

As Sir Leo went on to ask, "You must give me the name of your tailor," a voice said, "Do you remember me, Your Grace?"

The duke turned on his heel to find himself face-to-face with Lady Pamela Westcot, a woman who had caused his heart to have a good many palpitations in his youth. Amazingly, it appeared that maturity had enhanced her appearance.

Her hair was still the lustrous blonde he recalled, the eyes the wide, deep wondrous blue that had sent so many gentlemen mad for love of her. Her figure was as trim as he recalled, her sense of fashion still sure. The gown of cerulean blue satin, it seemed, could have suited only her. The neckline was as low as was possible without being considered immodest, and that did nothing to lessen her allure. The countess was aware, as he scrutinized her, that she presented a ravishing sight.

While the duke stared at her in wonderment, long hidden memories were being awakened. She smiled flirtatiously as she fluttered her fan, and at last he replied, "How could I possibly forget?"

Sir Leo murmured, "We can continue our coze at a more convenient time."

Giving a brief bow, he melted into the crowds, and Lady Westcot said with no further preamble, "What has brought you to London just now?"

"A desire to prove my sanity perhaps," he answered with a teasing smile.

She laughed dismissively. "Oh, that nonsense.

How could anyone who ever knew you believe it? In any event, you never cared a fig for what anyone said or thought of you. I don't believe you do now."

"You know me so well, my lady."

Her eyes were coy behind her fan, and he could easily imagine her lips pouting. "You used to call me Pammy."

Aware that their first meeting in years was being monitored carefully on all sides, he replied, "That was before we both acceded to our present positions."

"We are still the same people, are we not?"

"Are we?" he asked. She looked a little discomforted by his intense scrutiny, and then he added in a softer tone, "I was most distressed to hear of your sad loss."

Lady Westcot looked immediately woebegone. "It was a dreadful time. The shock! However, I feel I must now return to some semblance of normality, which is what my poor, dear Charlie would have wished."

"How very brave of you," he said gravely.

"My friends, who have been so very supportive, are making my return to full participation in society that much easier for me." She looked up at him, her blue eyes appealing. "I do so rely upon the support of those who care for me."

"There must be a legion of them, my lady." Her laugh was a little brittle, and he went on, glancing toward the dancers, "Will you do me the honor of standing up with me?"

The look she cast him was a provocative one. "We used to sport a toe so well together, but I regret I am engaged for the next three sets. However," she added, swishing her fan flirtatiously, "I am free for the first set after supper."

"I shall await the moment with impatience, I assure you."

As she walked away with the partner who had come to claim her for a cotillion, she cast him a longing look he recalled so well. He was fully aware her allure was as potent as that of a witch who could ensnare gentlemen in her spell when she set out to do so.

Before the duke could draw his gaze away from the vision of loveliness, her place at his side was taken by his sister, Meribel, accompanied by a handsome young man.

Seeing her frowning countenance, the duke said, "Is this not a delightful evening, Meribel?"

"It is tolerable enough," she allowed.

"This young man I suspect is my nephew, Dunsby."

The young man smiled. "Yes, Uncle Oliver. I'm obliged you remember me."

"I recall very well that you were an unpleasant fellow as a child, but I concede you appear to be much improved."

The young man grinned, and his mother commented, casting a resentful look in Lady Westcot's direction, "I observe that Westcot hussy has lost no time in reacquainting herself with you."

"I'm sure you'll agree it is always good to encounter old friends."

Lady Stanyon agreed to no such thing. "I note she has lost none of her inveigling ways, which gentlemen appear to appreciate."

"She has very pretty manners," the duke replied with maddening complacency.

Lady Stanyon was outraged, as her brother knew she would be. "Her husband has been dead for only six months."

"Because of that, we should all make an effort to extend to her our deepest sympathy, should we not, Meribel?"

"I am constantly amazed at how many gentlemen are forever showing her sympathy."

The duke suppressed his amusement and turned pointedly to his nephew. "Well, Dunsby, I hear you are now down from Oxford."

"Yes, Uncle, and about to take a color."

"Were you by any chance acquainted with my ward, Henry Turlington?"

"I know him slightly, but I'm afraid he was not timbered up to my weight."

The duke looked a little surprised. "Oh, why not?"

Dunsby appeared rather discomforted as he replied, "He was a trifle too worthy for my taste, and that of many others I must add. He preferred to work in his rooms rather than enjoy himself."

"Yes, I can understand why that would offend;" the duke replied dryly.

Dunsby Latchpole bowed slightly. "Excuse me, Mama, Uncle Oliver, I have engaged a lady to stand up with me for the next set."

Left alone with his elder sister, the duke said quickly before she could dispense one of her habitual set-downs, "Would you do me the honor, Meribel?"

Lady Stanyon smiled at last. "Gladly, Oliver."

As he led her to the dance floor, the duke conversed lightly. "I'm a little out of practice I'm afraid, so you'll have to excuse any mistakes I make. I shall try not to tread on your toes, naturally."

"Perhaps you should attend Henrietta's dancing classes."

He smiled wryly at the thought of sharing his niece's dancing master. Dryly he replied, "I don't believe that will be necessary."

"I will judge," she said imperiously.

"Betsey has insisted upon holding a party for me."

"I cannot believe Poor Betsey has insisted upon anything."

"I'm sure it will be a great effort for her, but that makes the invitation all the more precious, don't you think?"

Meribel Stanyon shook her head. "I dread to think what a mull she will make of it. I daresay, she is doing it at John's behest."

"Normally, I would agree with you, but on this occasion I don't believe it to be so."

"That is only because you do not know her as well as I do."

"I will not gainsay you on that score, Meribel, but I do believe, our sister-in-law may have hidden depths none of us know about."

Meribel Stanyon started to argue the point with him, but then she began to cluck her tongue. "Is something amiss?" her brother inquired.

"Dunsby! Trust my son to attend a female of no consequence whatsoever. I really must have words with him."

The duke transferred his attention to the young lady partnering his nephew, and although he knew he must accept his sister's opinion that the chit was of no consequence, he could see for himself she was no beauty.

When he returned his attention to his sister, he said, "Evidently she is one of this Season's debutantes."

"Poor child. One is obliged to feel a measure of pity, for she has a certain manner of address, but no countenance and little portion. I do not envy Mrs. Penrose's task in finding a husband for her daughter."

"Mrs. Penrose?" the duke repeated in shocked tones. "You did say the chit was a Miss Penrose?"

Lady Stanyon looked irritated by his interest. "You cannot possibly know them. They are people of little consequence and smaller fortune. I don't want Dunsby to become interested in her."

"I think it is more likely that his Aunt Valeria has asked him to show her some compassion."

When the music started up and the dance commenced, the duke could not help but watch Araminta Penrose, who was blissfully unaware of his interest in her. During the progress of the dance, he found himself facing her in the set and his reaction was one of great surprise despite Lady Dunwoody's warning, for she was most certainly far from the beauty Hal had lovingly described, and the duke could only assume that love had blinded him.

He assessed her critically and could find little to redeem her. Her hair was a mousy shade of brown and worn unfashionably long. Her figure was decidedly dumpy, and although her pink and silver gown was fashionable enough, this squab of a girl could not possibly do it justice. Facing her across the set, she smiled at him shyly. As she did so, her face suddenly became animated and her hazel eyes, her best feature the duke opined, were suddenly twinkling. However, after a moment she became discomforted by the intensity of his stare and averted her eyes, her cheeks coloring slightly.

When the dance ended, his sister hurried away, presumably to lecture her son on the folly of engaging poor, plain debutantes in dance. Supper was almost immediately announced, and seeing his sister-in-law in the midst of a milling throng making its way to the supper room, looking lost and alone, he accosted her.

"Betsey, allow me the honor of escorting you."

She blushed furiously, looked away, and desperately fiddled with her shawl. "How kind of you, but you mustn't allow me to keep you away from your friends, Oliver."

"I can't think of anyone I would rather be with just now," he assured her.

She blushed again and couldn't meet his eye. "I wish I had your way with words. You always contrive to say the right thing."

"Sometimes I mean it, too."

She laughed uncomfortably, and after he had assisted her in selecting some food from the ample buffet, he said, looking at her intently, "Does my brother treat you as he ought?"

Again she could not look directly at him. "Oh, indeed he does!"

"I do wonder about that at times, Betsey. You do deserve to be treated with respect. I know my brother well. I've known him for far longer than you, and there are times when his behavior leaves a great deal to be desired."

She smiled faintly. "You Barringtons are a proud

lot. It did his pride no good to be obliged to marry me."

"I knew some of his paramours, Betsey. He did well in marrying you, quite apart from your portion. He would do well to appreciate that."

"I realize that the arrival of new wealth into old families is sometimes resented as well as welcomed."

"Old families desperately need new blood in them," he pointed out.

With some difficulty she answered, "You are so kind to say so."

"I suspect that my sisters are also a trial to you."

"I wish I could be sophisticated, but I cannot be other than what I am."

"Then you do right not to let them change you."

"You're always kind to me and I appreciate it, but I don't mind, you see, if occasionally Johnny's attention strays. I am still Lady Elizabeth Barrington and always will be. That is what really matters."

"I hope so," the duke said doubtfully.

It appeared that their frank conversation had fired her with an unusual boldness, for she asked with no further preamble, "Is it true you have come back to pay court to Lady Westcot?"

His laughter was so loud, several groups of people stopped talking to stare at him. Betsey Barrington blushed furiously and murmured, "I do beg your pardon. I should not . . ."

"I don't mind your asking. Let the tattle-baskets do their worst. I shall only be amused, and as for Lady Westcot, I assure you I did not come back to pay court to her, for I didn't know she had been widowed. However, now that I am here . . ."

Betsey Barrington concentrated her gaze upon her supper. "Johnny is terrified you might marry and take up your place in the forefront of society. If you marry Lady Westcot, there will be no couple in the ton to equal you both."

The duke continued to look amused. "His concern is perfectly understandable, I suppose."

"I hope you do marry," she said with unusual fervor, "and open your house up to the beau monde."

"Why?" her brother-in-law asked in astonishment.

He caught sight then of Araminta Penrose in the midst of a group of young people. She was chattering unself-consciously, her plain face strangely animated. Whatever Hal felt for her, it was evident she was not languishing for love of him.

Lady Betsey glanced over her shoulders and noted his interest before she replied, "I would like you to be happy, Oliver."

He smiled knowingly. "I'm obliged to you for that, Betsey, but I rather believe you would enjoy Johnny getting a facer."

She blushed furiously at his perspicacity, and at that moment her husband joined them, his face flushed with drink. "Is my wife boring you with her prattle, Oliver?"

"No she is not, but you certainly are, Johnny."

His smiled faded and he muttered, "I'll warrant there is some truth in those rumors of lunacy. There's a full moon tonight."

As he wandered away, rather unsteadily, the duke returned his attention to his sister-in-law. "Does he regard everyone who converses with you a lunatic?"

She began to laugh, nodding her head as she did so. "Then I fear it is he who is deranged."

When he glanced once again in the direction of Araminta Penrose, who was now in conversation with an older woman, Lady Betsey asked, looking suddenly sly, "Would you like me to introduce you, Oliver?"

"Do you know that lady?"

"That is Mrs. Penrose and her daughter, Araminta."

"You would oblige me greatly by affecting an introduction, but don't jump to any untoward conclusions," he warned, and there was a twinkle in his eye.

Yet again she blushed furiously. "Your reason is of no account to me. I am only glad of an opportunity to be of service to you."

The two Penrose ladies were so intent upon their conversation, they did not see the duke until he was almost upon them, and then, when they did become aware of his proximity, both ladies looked alarmed.

Lady Betsey appeared no less flustered, regaining much of her usual shyness as she ventured, "Mrs. Penrose, Miss Araminta, allow me to introduce my brother-in-law, His Grace, the Duke of Avedon."

Mrs. Penrose immediately sketched a curtsy. Her daughter, however, seemed thunderstruck and could only stare at him as if mesmerized.

A moment later, she too sketched a curtsy before saying in a cold manner that, although expected, cut him nevertheless, "Your Grace, Mr. Turlington has spoken of you to me on many occasions."

"Kindly, I trust," he replied, injecting some warmth into his manner.

In fact, at that moment he felt irrationally angry with his ward for choosing so foolishly. He was angry with himself, too, for deigning to involve himself in such a paltry matter, which he recognized was only a result of his guilt. He was certain that if he had involved himself more with Hal during his formative years, he would not have been allowed to fall into the clutches of this dreadful young female.

The girl's lips seemed to curl before she replied, "I don't believe he could say an unkind word about anyone, nor perform an unkind deed."

"You evidently do not remember me, Your Grace," Mrs. Penrose broke in quickly, aware that her daughter's antagonism might well come to the fore with catastrophic results for all concerned.

The duke gazed at Mrs. Penrose for a moment or two before replying, "You are, I recall, a close friend of my sister, Lady Dunwoody, are you not?"

The woman's face became flushed with pleasure, "Lady Dunwoody has presented a delightful rout, has she not?"

"My sister has always possessed a knack of knowing how to entertain well," the duke agreed. A moment later, tiring of the stilted conversation that was going nowhere and might well go on indefinitely, he turned to Miss Penrose, who was tapping her folded fan impatiently against her knuckles. "Miss Penrose, would you do me the honor of standing up with me for one of the sets?"

As Mrs. Penrose bit her lip with apprehension, her daughter, who had been regarding him coldly throughout the conversation replied, "I regret to say, I cannot as I am fully engaged for the remainder of the evening."

Refusing to be nonplussed, he persisted, "That is a great pity, but I should very much like to have the opportunity to converse with you further."

"To what purpose?" Araminta asked icily.

Her demeanor was not such she could adequately convey a snub. He was fully aware of that and smiled to himself as he replied, "In order to discuss a matter of great import to both of us." Out of the corner of his eye, he observed his sister-in-law looking rather bewildered, but he could not help that. "I have been absent from town for so long, I had quite forgotten it is necessary to engage a young lady at the very outset of the evening if one is to stand any chance of finding her free."

From Miss Penrose's obdurate expression, it became evident to him that she was not in the least receptive to his charm, which he supposed he should have expected. He had judged her unseen as a scheming minx, and if that was true, he appreciated now she would not forgive him for thwarting what was perhaps her one chance of marrying comfortably.

"Nonetheless," the duke persisted, "mayhap you would do me the honor of accompanying me for a drive tomorrow afternoon?"

Before Araminta could snap out her refusal, her mother said, "Minty, dear, you were complaining you knew not where to go tomorrow afternoon. How kind of you to ask, Your Grace."

The girl looked mutinous and would yet have refused, except that the duke bowed quickly and went to seek out Lady Westcot for the promised dance.

"Mama, how could you?" Araminta said reproachfully as soon as he was out of earshot.

"Minty, you cannot possibly refuse an invitation from the Duke of Avedon. Is it not evident he is in a fidge to talk to you about Mr. Turlington?"

The girl continued to look mutinous, and Lady Betsey, completely mistaking the situation, timidly ventured. "I know my brother-in-law has an awesome reputation and can appear stiff-rumped, and even arrogant at times, but you must not be afraid of him. You will find him diverting company."

Mrs. Penrose and her daughter exchanged meaningful looks, but made no attempt to disagree with her. Mrs. Penrose remained concerned about her daughter when, as soon as Araminta was able to give herself a respite from all that was happening in the ballroom, she wandered into the card room. Some of the guests were playing dice, and when one gentleman laughingly suggested that Araminta take part, she needed no further encouragement to do so, winning, much to everyone's surprise.

"Beginner's luck," Lord John Barrington suggested slyly.

Araminta smiled. "Yes, I daresay it is, so I shall depart now with my winnings."

"That is most unsportsmanlike," one gentleman chided.

"It is indeed foolish of me not to want to continue until I have lost everything," she responded, "but foolish I must be. Good evening, gentlemen."

Taking their place on the dance floor some time later, Lady Westcot looked up at her partner from beneath her long lashes and murmured soothingly, "My poor Avedon to partake of supper in such dull company. You should have excused yourself and joined our little party—all your old acquaintances, my dear."

"Sometimes it is necessary to seek such companions," he told her smilingly, "for if I was to spend all my time in dazzling company, I might before long be blinded."

Her laughter rang out loud and clear, causing Araminta to cast the handsome couple a ferocious look.

FIVE

"He was not at all as I imagined him to be," Araminta Penrose admitted to her mother the following day.

Mrs. Penrose, who up until that moment appeared intent upon her sewing, looked up and smiled faintly. "What did you expect, my dear? Horns and a forked tail?"

"You may well jest, Mama, but I confess it was a relief not to discern any sign of lunacy."

Araminta gazed out into the street from her position at a small table where she had been until that moment, concentrating upon cutting silhouettes from pieces of paper.

"However, that does not leave Hal any legal alternative."

"I told you that was a Banbury Tale. How anyone could believe it, was beyond my reason. In my opinion, there is a great deal of truth in the notion he has come to see Lady Westcot. It was noted by many of us that he was attentive to her."

"The same could be said of his attention to me, Mama," Araminta pointed out, much to her mother's discomfiture. Then she sighed. "It is such a vexing situation. Sometimes I feel it is intolerable. The duke is being so unjust."

71

"You must acknowledge that being a guardian of a young man of means is a burdensome thing," Mrs. Penrose ventured, attending her sewing once again.

Araminta had returned to snipping silhouettes, but she paused to reply, "Mayhap, but Hal has not exactly acted the rip, and I believe the duke's refusal is more like to be because he is too high in the instep. The Penroses aren't up to the knocker."

"Minty, dearest, I beg of you not to be so vulgar in your speech. It is not at all ladylike."

"No doubt His Grace, the Duke of Avedon, believes me to be vulgar, so I might as well live up to his expectations."

"I thought he was rather charming. He did not cut us, although I am a trifle disappointed he did not recall our previous acquaintanceship before I reminded him of it."

Araminta frowned ferociously at the silhouette she was fashioning with her scissors. "He is a treacherously odious man. One only has to witness the manner in which that family treats Lady Betsey."

"His Grace always treats her with the utmost charm and consideration."

"I wouldn't trust that charm one jot, Mama. I just cannot understand why you insist upon championing that man."

"I just wish you to see the matter from his standpoint, dearest. You are bound to confess, are you not, you are a mite partisan."

"As you should be, and I do wish you hadn't forced me to go driving with him this afternoon. Spending so much time in his company is outside of enough. I am in a quake every time I think about it."

"I would have thought you would welcome the opportunity to try and change his mind about the wedding."

"I doubt if any entreaty I might make to him will succeed, Mama, and it is not in my nature to bend at the knee."

She snipped at the paper aggressively, as if attacking the duke himself, and her mother said mischievously, "Lady Betsey declares every female in London would give her most valuable tiara to ride in His Grace's new curricle."

Araminta cast her mother a disgusted look. "Not I, Mama. In any event, I do not possess a tiara, well only Grandmother Fletcher's and that is not so splendid."

"Driving with the Duke of Avedon will do you nothing but good. It will possibly make you the toast of the town. No one save Lady Dunwoody has paid us any attention since your debut, but everyone will be obliged to acknowledge you after today."

"Oh, do not say so, Mama!"

"You need not doubt it. Your Season may yet be a great success."

Araminta could not help but laugh. "That would be most ironic."

Thoughtfully Mrs. Penrose went on, "You must own he is as handsome as ever he was."

"I confess only that he is much aware of his own consequence."

"He was always a fine figure of a man."

"I cannot join in the general admiration of the man, and furthermore I vow he shall not be allowed to gammon me with his Spanish coin!"

The ormolu mantel clock chimed the half hour,

and Mrs. Penrose ventured, "Minty, dearest, you must make haste to change your clothes. It would not do to keep His Grace waiting for you."

"I refuse to act like some of the hen-witted bread-and-butter misses I have observed, casting sheep's eyes at him, which is, no doubt, what he would wish."

Mrs. Penrose sighed. "I only trust you are able to keep a civil tongue in your head for the duration of your ride together."

"You may be sure I will not beg him to relent whatever the temptation. The Penroses have as much pride as His Grace's family, even though we don't possess such great consequence."

Her mother smiled understandingly. "Go along, dearest, and show His Grace that Araminta Penrose has great breeding."

Reluctantly, the young lady got to her feet and set aside her scissors and paper from which she had fashioned a grotesque cartoon of the duke. "I don't suppose there is any manner in which I can cry off, unless I pretend to fall victim of an ague . . ."

"Minty!" her mother protested, and she sighed again, "I just hope I shall not be goaded into some sharp retort in the time I am obliged to endure his company," she declared as she left the room, leaving her mother to frown worriedly after her.

Although she had no wish to go driving with the Duke of Avedon, Araminta took time to choose her outfit very carefully indeed. There was no doubt he had invited her to talk about his ward and her connection with him, and not for the usual reason, which was a desire to be in the company of a dashing female.

When she was informed of the duke's arrival, she felt incredibly nervous. Earlier, anger and resentment of what she regarded his unfair intransigence had dominated her emotions where the duke was concerned. Now that she recognized there might well be a chance of making him reconsider, she was in a quake, feeling unequal to the task. If it was possible to succeed where Hal had failed, it would be worth enduring his company, for the drive was bound to be observed by many, as her mother had predicted, and draw her into the forefront of the beau monde's attention, something she had so far striven hard to avoid.

Looking into the cheval glass in some dismay, she tied the ribbons of her most stylish bonnet and sighed deeply. There was nothing she could do to improve the looks nature had bestowed upon her, although she knew full well a beautiful woman could achieve with gentle persuasion what others have no chance of attaining. Although she had never had cause to lament her lack of classical beauty before, now she most certainly did. The green ruched satin that lined the fashionable poke brim of her bonnet accentuated the green flecks in her wide hazel eyes; but still she despaired about her powers over gentlemen. She had no notion how to wheedle or ingratiate herself, and it was too late to acquire the skills now.

As she walked down the stairs, her back was straight and her head held high. She was very much aware of the imposing figure of the duke awaiting her in the hall below, and all at once Araminta understood his alarming reputation. He appeared quite formidable as she walked toward him, tall and dark, clad in a caped driving coat that reached his ankles, a high-crowned beaver clasped in his hands. Most disturbing was the way he was regarding her, with such serious consideration. How inferior he must find her compared to high-flyers like Lady Pamela Westcot, whom he would more normally wish to ride with in his splendid new carriage.

When she reached the bottom of the stairs, his face relaxed into a smile, and he came forward to take her hand briefly in his. "Miss Penrose, how charming you look. That shade of green suits you admirably."

Despite her hostile attitude toward him, she found his charm effective, and to her chagrin, she began to blush. It was plain to see how easily he could disarm less prejudiced females with his charm.

"You are very kind to say so, Your Grace," she murmured, and then she turned to the footman on duty in the hall, handing him a letter. "Please have this dispatched without delay."

Immediately she returned her attention to the duke, who escorted her out into the afternoon sunshine. When he handed her into the curricle, she could not help but admire it. Compared to the more modest and slightly old-fashioned chariots driven by Hal and the other gentlemen of her acquaintance, it was quite the smartest she had ever seen, and she began to understand a little why Hal was so much in awe of his guardian.

After the duke had climbed up beside her and taken the ribbons from his tiger, they set off. Araminta thrust her hands into her muff, which she rested tensely in her lap.

Once he had set the horses into a gentle trot, he

glanced at her unyielding profile. "Do you enjoy your stay in London, Miss Penrose?"

"It is tolerable," she replied without returning his glance.

"It is more usual to hear ecstatic declarations from the lips of a recent debutante rather than such lukewarm enthusiasm."

"It is difficult to be enthusiastic when one's heart is engaged elsewhere." He cast her a questioning look, during which her cheeks grew rather pink, and then she added, her eyes downcast, "There is someone I miss dreadfully at Middlehampton."

After a considering pause, he asked rather abruptly, "Do you often go riding in the Park, Miss Penrose?"

"Occasionally I have hired a hack and ridden early in the morning, when the mist still covers the fields, simply because that reminds me of home."

"That must be very pleasurable, but I meant, do you often ride at the fashionable hour as we are about to do?"

"Sometimes Mama and I stroll along the Grand Strut on a pleasant afternoon, but we do not often drive or ride."

"Surely you must occasionally drive along with an admirer."

She looked at him at last, at his strong profile, the lips curved into a slight smile, and she wondered if he was, in fact, setting a trap for her to fall into. Concealing her contempt for him was one thing, not making the position worse was quite another.

"No, Your Grace," she answered at last.

"I can scare believe you do not have a score of admirers vying for your company, ma'am."

"Believe what you wish, Your Grace, but I did not come to town either in the hope I would attract an admirer or expecting to do so."

"How long have you known my ward, Miss Penrose?" he asked abruptly a moment later.

Araminta started slightly and pushed her hands even farther into her muff so they should not shake. "Since we were very young."

"You live close by one another, do you not?"

"Our homes are only a few miles apart. There are several large estates in the Middlehampton area. We all visit each other socially, and the children inevitably grew up together. Hal learned to dance with us."

He paused to glance at her, frowning slightly. "You are evidently much attached to my ward, Miss Penrose."

Araminta sighed deeply and refused to look at him. "Yes."

"It is apparent to me Hal has matured into a young man with few vices."

"If he possesses any," she replied, "they are not apparent to me."

The duke smiled grimly. "Your stay in London must have provided you with a number of shocks. Gentlemen in general are not so angelic."

She fixed him with a cold stare. "I am not so green, I did not already know that."

They had come to the Prince of Wales gate, and he slowed the carriage to accommodate all the others who were streaming into Hyde Park at that time.

A moment later, he returned his attention to her. "You evidently consider me unreasonable in my attitude. I would like to take this opportunity of explaining it to you."

Araminta looked at him then, sensing that if this conversation were to continue in this vein, the afternoon was most likely to end in tears, so she said in a less than steady voice, "It is kind of you to invite me to ride with you, Your Grace, and I do hope to enjoy the experience, but I would be obliged if you would not engage me in conversation regarding Mr. Turlington, for mention of that matter, which concerns the both of us, distresses me beyond all bounds."

"I do beg your pardon, ma'am," the duke responded, looking both surprised and a little taken aback.

"If you expected me to beg and plead with you to relent, I must disappoint you. I shall do no such thing, so let there be an end to the discussion. Any amount of explanation will not satisfy me."

The duke took several seconds to reply. "Very well, Miss Penrose," he said at last. "It shall be as you wish, only I did think, by your attitude toward me yesterday evening, you might wish to speak of your feelings on the matter, which I accept are exceedingly profound."

"There are some feelings which must needs remain private" were her final words on the subject.

He inclined his head in acknowledgment of her wishes, and it was then that Araminta began to notice the interest being directed toward the curricle. Naturally, she was aware of the reason for it. The Duke of Avedon had always attracted great interest in all he did, but it was far more intense now he had returned to town in the wake of all those rumors about him. No one expected to see a nonpareil such as he to be seen driving with a drab like her. Araminta possessed no illusions about herself. Only a fortune could elevate her, and her father did not possess that.

"You have put to a team of four," she pointed out, "and yet you cannot possibly drive with any speed in the Park with so many other carriages around."

"I confess it is an affectation, although I do not just drive here, where it is congested, with a fetching female at my side for all to see."

Her cheeks grew slightly pink at the compliment, although she knew better than to believe his flattery. He was too practiced a tongue-pad to deceive her, and she feared he must know it, too, which was bound to invoke further dislike and disapproval.

Fortunately the attention of the two passengers was caught by the sight of Lady Pamela Westcot coming toward them in the distinctive shell-shaped carriage belonging to "Romeo" Coates, a vastly wealthy dandy of the duke's slight acquaintance.

Lady Westcot called, "Good day," as the carriages came abreast of each other, but she looked rather displeased despite all the attention she was receiving.

Both Araminta and the duke inclined their heads before he said, "The greatest pleasure of a drive in the Park is who one encounters."

"I am not so certain I am able to agree with you, Avedon," the countess responded archly, casting another glance at Araminta.

The duke did not rise to that declaration. Instead he asked, "How fitting your conveyance. An exotic shell for a perfect pearl."

She looked more pleased then, and the dandy

laughed. "You've lost none of your expertise as a tongue-pad, Avedon, not that I would expect you would. Good to see you again. London will be a little more colorful now, I fancy."

"It could not be more colorful than when you are here, Coates," the duke responded with a laugh.

A shout of "Cockle-doodle-do!" arrested the dandy, and with a brief farewell, he drove on.

"Why does everyone shout that to him?" Araminta asked as they drove on a moment afterward.

"Because he is larger than life, and his family motto is 'While I live, I crow!' He makes every effort to live up to the motto, as you might have noticed."

He was smiling quite genuinely now. To Araminta, he seemed all at once much more human and even likable, but she knew she must maintain her guard. He was her enemy, and she must never forget that, however affable he might seem. No doubt the encounter with Lady Westcot had caused the change in him. Araminta could not help but feel a little resentment over that, but acknowledged it was so.

No sooner had Romeo Coates driven away with his beautiful passenger, than Lord John Barrington could be seen approaching in his midnight blue high-perch phaeton. He, too, was accompanied by a beautiful woman, this one Araminta did not recognize.

All at once the duke's affability faded as quickly as it had come, and a cold, hard look came into his eyes, reminding his companion that he could be other than charming and pleasant. She didn't doubt that this was the side of the duke's character Hal had witnessed when he had visited Summerhills not long ago.

In spite of his brother's frowning countenance, Lord John was all affability as he greeted them. "Avedon! How splendid to see you enjoying every diversion, just as you used to."

He glanced curiously at Araminta, who inclined her head in his direction, but she was more interested in the ravishing creature sitting up beside him. Araminta felt she was no older than herself, but she was exquisitely dressed, and she positively envied her high-poke bonnet, the style of which was only recently featured in the *Ladies' Monthly Museum.* Araminta could not help but admire her style.

The duke nodded curtly, and to Araminta's surprise, ignored the female at his brother's side. In the face of the duke's uncommunicative attitude, Lord John said, his cheerfulness becoming a little strained. "The plan for our little soiree is well in hand."

"Good day, John," his brother said, and drove on with no further ado.

"The lady is a great beauty," Araminta commented as they drove on, curious about his attitude.

"My brother invariably seeks out companions who are pleasing to the eye and flattering to his image."

"Do not most gentlemen?"

He turned to cast her a strange look before he flicked the whip over the backs of his team. They went a little faster, but not nearly as fast as they were capable of going. Araminta sensed the frustration in him for not being able to drive at some speed because of the congestion in the Park. There was a good deal of suppressed anger in his manner that discomforted her somewhat.

She noted that they were driving toward one of the gates, almost ignoring countless people anxious for the duke to stop and have a word. For some reason, his encounter with Lord John had displeased him, and Araminta did not know what to say. Lady Westcot, she was sure, would know how to calm him with a few well-chosen words.

Lady Stanyon, driving along in a barouche with her sister and Cleo, turned to Lady Dunwoody and asked, "Wasn't that Avedon I saw driving away just then?"

Her sister smiled faintly. "It looks very much like his new curricle."

"I do wonder if we might be mistaken, for who is the drab of a girl beside him?"

"It looks like Miss Penrose, Meribel. Araminta Penrose." When her sister appeared bewildered, she added, "Bella Penrose's daughter."

Lady Stanyon's puzzlement turned to surprise. "How odd. Avedon must have changed drastically, but that still is most uncharacteristic of him." She drew a sigh and smiled. "At least I am glad to note he was not accompanied by Pamela Westcot. That would be outside of enough!"

"I cannot understand your hostility toward Pammy, Meribel. I think she is well suited to our brother."

"Fustian! That mantrap is not in the least suited to our brother, although I understand why *you* insist upon taking color with her. She is a crony of yours, is she not?"

"So is Bella Penrose."

"Why do so many gentlemen insist upon choosing wives who are plainly not suited to them, and females are just as foolish to accept their offers."

"I don't believe our brother is about to offer for anyone. Anyone who expects him to return to Summerhills with a bride is very likely to be disappointed."

Meribel Stanyon's eyes narrowed. "What do you know of the matter, Valeria?"

Lady Dunwoody assumed an innocent expression. "Nothing, Meribel, I assure you, only I do not believe our brother has come to town in search of a bride."

The marchioness looked thoughtful as they drove on. Meanwhile the object of their interest had arrived back in Berkeley Street and was handing Araminta down from the carriage. It was a great relief to her, although being in the duke's company had not been as unpleasant as she had expected. Mainly, she suspected, because she had refused to attempt to argue him out of his intransigence.

In fact, the interest aroused by her presence in the Duke of Avedon's curricle was unexpectedly pleasant. For the first time in her life, people of consequence were taking note of her. No one had expected her to have a remarkable Season—that was for heiresses and beauties—not that she wanted to be one of their number, but to be so honored in others' eyes was momentarily, at least, gratifying. She just hoped Hal wouldn't come to hear of it, or if he did, he would understand her motives.

"Thank you for your condescension, Your Grace," she murmured as he relinquished her hand.

"It was my pleasure, ma'am," he replied, "although we did not have the discussion we ought."

"Oh dear," she murmured, affecting dismay, "I did so hope you invited me for my own sake rather than because of my acquaintanceship with Mr. Turlington."

The duke was not in the least hoodwinked by her words, and he smiled wryly. "Next time, I vow I shall, but mayhap we can still indulge in that little coze on another occasion."

"This is not some trifling matter on which a gentleman can wager a few guineas in his club," she could not help but retort. "Will permission be granted? Won't it? I'll wager a pony that it won't! This concerns the future lives and happiness of human beings."

He looked a little discomforted by her sudden and unexpected ardor. "Then you really should allow me to explain to you my reservations that, I'm sure, you will not find so unreasonable."

"It is useless for you to waste your time in such a discourse, Your Grace. I do not doubt for one moment you have what you regard as valid reasons for being so cruel toward a young man in whom you have showed precious little interest in the last few years, but I am persuaded I should not understand them, however persuasively you detailed them to me!"

A cold look came into his eyes while she spoke, and Araminta knew she had gone too far, just as she had feared she might. He was not a man who liked to be gainsaid on any score, especially by a female, and she recalled what her mother had said about his temper. Because of his alarming reputation, she suspected few would dare to question his ideas and decisions, however outrageous and unfair. But now that she had challenged his authority and, worse, pointed out his failing, she was certain all was lost. Any chance of changing his mind had effectively been sabotaged by her own outspokeness, and Araminta had rarely felt so wretched.

"Your frankness is refreshing, ma'am," he murmured.

Then he bowed stiffly in response to her brief curtsy before she walked quickly back to the house. When she reached the door, she paused to glance back and discovered he was still standing on the pavement, staring at her, and she hurried inside the moment the door was opened.

When she heard the curricle departing a few moments later, she drew a deep sigh of regret. As Araminta had feared, she had made a mull of the entire episode.

SIX

When the duke returned to his house in Piccadilly, he was definitely out of sorts. Her set-down had infuriated him. No one had ever spoken to him in such a manner before, and for it to come from such a slip of a girl was outrageous. How dare she question his very reasonable behavior? he fumed.

To his chagrin, Araminta Penrose had proved to be quite different to how he had envisaged her, and the outing had not turned out in the least as he had intended. The girl he had imagined Hal's beloved to be would have accepted his reasons, and even agreed with him, with no further ado. The beautiful but foolish heiress Hal's description had conjured up in his mind was in reality plain, poor, but with unexpected mettle. Although he had not wanted his ward to marry a green girl at so young an age, now he wished Araminta had proved to be that type. He would have much preferred it.

More than ever the duke felt that Hal had not chosen wisely, and he, too, ought to come to London to mix more freely with other young ladies, rather than be inveigled into wedlock by the one strong-willed female whose only chance of a good match this was.

The moment he had been divested of his outer

clothing, a letter was handed to him. It had been forwarded from Summerhills, and the duke immediately recognized Hal's spidery hand. He hurried into the study and broke the wafer, scanning the sheet eagerly. If he had hoped for some measure of repentance in his ward, he was immediately disappointed.

Your Grace, the letter began, and the duke was immediately stung by his ward's deliberate formality. *Since my visit to Summerhills, I hope you have had time to reflect upon the unjust way you treated my most reasonable request for permission to marry the only woman I will ever love. Once again, I implore you to reconsider and grant us the happiness we crave. Yours ever respectfully, Henry Turlington.*

The duke smiled grimly as he crumpled the sheet and pitched it into the fire. Then he sat down at the desk, and picking up his quill, he began to write.

My dear Hal, I have, as you requested quite reasonably, considered the matter on which we conversed at great length at Summerhills. In addition, I have been investigating the matter and must conclude that my original decision must stand for the time being. Furthermore, I entreat you to join me in town at the earliest moment, so you may broaden your acquaintance with others of your age.

He signed it with his flowing hand, sealed the parchment with the Avedon seal of a lion encircled by oak leaves—the motto *Ever Valiant*—and handed it to a footman for immediate dispatch to Mapplewood.

When that was done, he flung himself into a high-backed chair close to the fire and tried to concentrate on a book chosen from his extensive library. However, he could not concentrate and eventually gave up. After prowling around the room for a few minutes, his brow furrowed and deep in thought, his face cleared, and he rang for a footman.

"Your Grace?" the lackey inquired.

"Would you locate Timmins and send him to me, Fowler?"

"Yes, Your Grace."

It was a rather impatient wait for the duke until his head groom finally arrived, and when he did, the man entered the study hesitantly, fingering his hat in a nervous gesture.

"Ah, Timmins," the duke greeted him heartily. "Come along in."

"Is something amiss, Your Grace?"

"I think not, but I do have one or two questions to put to you."

The man looked no less uncomfortable as he replied, "Ask away, Your Grace, and I'll do my level best to answer."

"You were, I recollect, seeing, if that is the word, a maidservant from a household in Berkeley Street. Is that correct?"

The man looked even more concerned now. "I never did anything! If she's trying to cut me up . . ."

The duke held up one hand. "No, no, I assure you, Timmins, nothing of the sort has come to my knowledge. If it did, is it likely I would concern myself?" The groom looked a little less anxious, but still remained concerned. "Now, where exactly is this servant girl employed?"

The groom continued to finger his hat nervously. "There's the two of them now, Your Grace," he answered at last and with some evident difficulty.

The duke's eyebrows rose a little as he answered

wryly. "Really, Timmins, I believe I give you too much free time, if that is the way you conduct yourself."

"You can be sure, I don't neglect my duties, Your Grace, not the one of them."

"That is true, but what I wonder, what would Mrs. Timmins, hard at work at Summerhills, make of it?"

The groom looked alarmed anew. "Oh, you wouldn't tell her, would you, Your Grace?"

"Indeed, I would not! What do you take me for? We gentlemen must keep our counsel on such matters. Now, which households employ these females?"

"The Buckinghams at number fifty-three and Lady Nayler at forty-seven."

"I am all admiration, Timmins. As far as I recall, the houses almost face each other across the street."

"If anything, that makes it easier, Your Grace."

Still smiling, the duke said, "Mrs. Penrose lives at number sixty-five."

"Yes, Your Grace."

"I'm sure it is possible for a man of your address and proven ability to become acquainted with some female employed there."

The groom looked startled. "Your Grace?"

"I think I had better explain."

"I wish you would, Your Grace, for it's certain I don't know what you're getting at. I'm in a pretty case of pickles as it is."

The duke laughed and said, "I've never found myself so fortunate."

"It's hard, Your Grace, very hard."

"I'm sure it is," the duke replied, still looking amused. "I don't know whether to envy or to pity you. However, I digress. The truth of the matter is, Timmins, it would be advantageous to know as much about the social life of Miss Araminta Penrose as is possible. Do you follow my drift?"

"Perfectly, Your Grace."

"You will find me most grateful for anything you are able to discover."

"Rely upon me, Your Grace. I won't fail you."

When he had gone, the duke began to doubt the wisdom of what he had put in train, for he felt, in all truth, he need have nothing more to do with Miss Araminta Penrose, but he had always valued Hal Turlington's friendship and admiration, and he did not wish to appear churlish or unreasonable. Hal was in love and could see no wrong in the chosen one. It was up to him as a guardian to prove that Miss Penrose was not suitable as a bride. If proof was available, it would be found.

Since applying himself to restoring the family fortunes, the duke had prided himself upon his resourcefulness, which would be equally useful on this occasion.

His reverie was interrupted by a footman bearing a silver salver. The duke stared at the invitation, which was to the promised soiree to be held in his honor by his brother and sister-in-law.

"There is not much chance of avoiding this one," he said out loud, tossing it back on the salver.

Almost immediately the footman had withdrawn, another arrived to announce that Lady Stanyon was without. Choking back a gasp of irritation, he ordered her to be shown in and forced a smile to his face as he greeted her with a kiss on each cheek.

"Meribel, my dear, how nice to see you again."

"Don't give me your flummery, Oliver," she replied as she sat down and began to strip off her gloves. "However, I own it is good to be back in Avedon House again. I thought if I waited for an invitation, I should be obliged to wait until I am too old and infirm to be able to take advantage of it."

"Meribel, when I issue invitations of any sort, it will only be because *you* have agreed to be my hostess."

Lady Stanyon looked momentarily taken aback, and then unusually pleased. "I should like that, Oliver. It would be like it used to be when I was hostess for Papa."

"Shall I order you tea?"

"No, I thank you. I took tea with Rosie Claypool before coming here. If one wants to hear the latest *on-dits*, Rosie Claypool is the lady who will have them. I thought she might even be able to tell me something about *you*, and your reason for coming to town."

The duke ignored her heavy sarcasm, and when he seated himself, she glanced around. "Where have all the paintings come from? I thought they'd all gone to pay Papa's debts."

"Most of them did. We lost a great many treasures, which I have been at pains to replace in the past few years."

For once Lady Stanyon looked impressed. "How clever of you, my dear."

"Since arriving in London, I've visited various auction rooms, including Mr. Christie's in Pall Mall. I hope to make this house as fine as it used to be when we were children."

"How splendid of you, Oliver, for I would not have

thought it possible. How did you contrive to achieve such a transformation?"

"I had little hope of repurchasing all Papa was obliged to sell to pay his debts as well as those I had to dispose of, but I think I have done well nevertheless. It was mortifying for me to be obliged to purchase the Zoffany portrait of Mama sitting with us all as children, but at least it is back in the family again."

"I'm so glad you did contrive, Oliver. It still angers me whenever I visit Lord and Lady Ridgeley's house to see the Gainsborough painting of Mama in their gallery."

"It's no longer there, Meribel." When she looked at him in surprise, he went on to explain, "I visited the Ridgeleys a few months ago and made them a substantial offer for the Gainsborough. It's at Summerhills, and you may see it whenever you wish. For every Rubens, Titian, and so on we were obliged to sell, I have purchased another. If you have time, I'll show you around the house."

"Another time, Oliver, it will be my pleasure. I own you have done well, my dear."

The duke smiled wryly. "Coming from you, Meribel, I take that as extravagant praise."

Lady Stanyon toyed with one of her rings for a moment before confessing, "I caught sight of you driving in Hyde Park this afternoon."

"I beg your pardon for not seeing *you*."

"It is not so surprising. The Park always is so crowded at that time." She laughed gruffly. "I cannot conceive why we go."

"For the same reason as everyone else, my dear— to see and be seen."

"I say it is as well," Lady Stanyon replied, reverting to her more usual asperity, "otherwise I should not know what is going on with my own brother."

The duke sat back in the chair, his hands resting lightly on the arms. "Nothing is going on, Meribel," he said in a warning tone, "so do not seek to make a case of pickles out of something that is a nothing."

His sister sat forward. "When the Duke of Avedon is seen at the fashionable hour driving a nondescript dab of a girl in Hyde Park, one is bound to wonder, and I am not alone in that."

The duke smiled artlessly. "There is no need for anyone to wonder."

"She is not in the least your style, Oliver."

"No, I grant you, she is not that, Meribel."

The marchioness sat back and frowned. "It is not in the least like you to waste your time with a dab of a debutante. You cannot in the least blame me for wondering what is going on."

The duke drew an almost imperceptible sigh. "Miss Penrose's mother is a crony of Valeria's. Didn't you know?"

For a moment, Lady Stanyon was taken aback, and then realization dawned. "I see. Valeria must have solicited your help to promote the chit's chances, for it is evident she has none at present. One needs either beauty or wealth, preferably both, otherwise a Season is usually a useless exercise, however good-natured the girl. But I am bound to say, it is not in the least like you to be so accommodating to your sister, or indeed to green girls just come out."

"You just do not appreciate the finer side to my nature, Meribel," he answered, casting her an urbane smile.

It was her turn to look wry. "I believe I know you all too well, my dear."

The duke was afraid his sister spoke the truth on that score. For part of his childhood, she had been forced to adopt the role of surrogate mother to him and the other two siblings in the family. As a consequence, there was little he could hide from her.

"You are naturally well aware of the *on-dits* currently circulating the drawing rooms, aren't you?"

The duke cast her a bland look. "Is there one in particular you wish to bring to my attention?"

The marchioness bit back her impatience and said in clipped tones, "I refer in particular to the one regarding you and Lady Pamela Westcot."

"Ah, *that* one."

"Oliver, don't seek to gammon me. It is mortifying to have people of long acquaintance refer to the matter, and not be able to answer with any certainty what I hope is the truth."

"And what do you hope is the truth, Meribel?"

"That she no longer means anything to you."

The duke got up and began to prowl around the room. "If I told you I did not return to pay court to Lady Westcot, would you believe me?"

"I believe you would be one of the few gentlemen, married or not, who is not in pursuit of that creature. I do trust you are not in earnest over her, Oliver."

"She has lost none of her allure, I grant you."

"I wonder what it is about gentlemen who vie for a beauty's favor? It is as if they are hit with a collective lunacy."

"Then no one should be surprised if I join in the madness."

"I just trust you recall at all times, she once broke your heart and is like to do so again."

"My heart was only bruised a little," he admitted, casting her a smile, "or mayhap it was only my pride. In any event, it did me no lasting harm, I assure you."

"You're just roasting me, Oliver, but I'd like you to know, I shall never, never forgive you if you make that flip-flap the Duchess of Avedon. There, I have said what I wished."

Her lips clamped shut, and the duke once again drew a sigh. "I am in an invidious position, Meribel. If I were to marry Lady Westcot, you would not forgive me, and if I do not, Valeria won't forgive me. What is a fellow to do?"

Lady Stanyon got to her feet and began to pull on her gloves. "I leave it entirely to your good sense."

When she had gone, he ran his fingers through his carefully arranged locks. The solitude of Summerhills was very inviting at that moment, and he contemplated setting out for the country at once. But because he had never run away from any situation, he immediately resolved to remain awhile longer. He owed that much to Hal.

Meanwhile, not far away in Grosvenor Square, Lady Betsey Barrington was preparing for dinner when the door to her boudoir opened, and she was surprised to see her husband in the doorway. He was dressed for dinner and looked both immaculate and handsome. Her heart leaped a little as it invariably did when she saw him.

"May I have words with you, my dear?" he asked. She nodded, and the maidservant who had been attending her, scuttled away. "I've been thinking about the soiree we are holding in Avedon's honor, Betsey . . ."

She watched him through the mirror. "I have it in hand, dearest. There is nothing for you to concern yourself about."

"Of course there is! Everything must be perfect on this occasion."

"It will be, Johnny."

He looked at her in some surprise. "I thought it might be best if you consulted with my sisters on the matter of who to invite."

"There is no need for me to consult with anyone. As I said, I have the matter entirely in hand."

Somewhat taken aback by her uncharacteristic certainty, he smiled foolishly. "You cannot contrive on your own, Betsey. You know full well you cannot."

His wife looked unusually stubborn. "I can, Johnny. I assure you, I can contrive very well indeed. There is no need to trouble either Lady Stanyon or Lady Dunwoody."

He paused to rest his hands on her shoulders. "I trust that you have taken the utmost care with the invitation list, for it is most important. We must show the utmost respect to my brother, but it is even more essential for us to do all we can to ensure he retains his bachelor status."

"Why?"

He laughed disparagingly. "I should have thought the reason was evident."

"Is it not enough that you are Lord John Barrington?"

"No! Avedon has never cared for such matters, but I do."

"Recall that I am an outsider. I don't understand

such things. What does it matter if your brother takes up his rightful place in the forefront of society?"

"You have always harbored a fondness for Avedon, haven't you, my dear?"

"He has always exhibited the utmost kindness to me."

"Yes, his charm encompasses even you, Betsey. If you'd been a beauty, who knows? With your fortune, you might today be the Duchess of Avedon, but my brother always required more than mere wealth in a female. No one is a greater arbiter of beauty than he."

Lady Betsey blinked away a tear. "I only ever wanted you, Johnny."

He squeezed her shoulders as he stepped back. "Then you have much cause to be content."

When he walked toward the door, she turned quickly to look at him directly at last. "Are you dining at home tonight?"

He cast her a faint smile. "I regret not, my dear. I am engaged to dine at my club, so I'll bid you good night."

When he had gone once again, she blinked away a tear before clipping on a diamond bracelet with a definite snap. Then she drew out of a drawer the guest list she had carefully made out, and glanced down the columns of names featured on it. As she locked it away once again, she smiled oddly, and then she got to her feet and walked out of her boudoir and down to her solitary meal.

SEVEN

On the way to the soiree at Lord and Lady John Barrington's house, Araminta was unusually quiet. Her mother glanced at her curiously several times before venturing, "You have spoken very little of your drive with His Grace, Minty."

The girl appeared a little preoccupied and started slightly at the sound of her mother's voice. "There is so little to report, Mama, save that it was not as unpleasant as I had expected, although I cannot vouch for His Grace agreeing with me."

"You had the opportunity to converse a good deal during the drive."

"You know full well what it is like at that hour in Hyde Park. We were stopping every minute to speak to others, and I informed His Grace categorically that I did not wish to discuss Henry Turlington with him."

"I thought your objective was to do just that."

"Originally I had hoped so, but, Mama, I am not in the least clever or sophisticated, and I realized I could not adequately argue on the injustice of the situation with him. I did not above all other considerations wish to make matters worse."

"That's not possible. How could matters be worse than they are now?"

"Hal wouldn't wish to be on bad terms with his guardian, now or in the future."

"In any event," Mrs. Penrose went on in a brighter tone, "I'm persuaded your drive with the Duke of Avedon has resulted in several invitations to diversions in very elevated circles! It has done you nothing but good."

"I daresay," Araminta replied with rather less enthusiasm. "It will be ironic, will it not, if my name is now being linked by the tattle-baskets to that of the Duke of Avedon?"

A peal of laughter escaped her mother. "What nonsense that is!"

"Indeed," her daughter responded darkly. Then she added, "We encountered Lady Pamela Westcot in the Park. She was with Romeo Coates in his fantastic carriage, and she looked quite breathtaking."

"When does she not?"

"His Grace had good reason to be with me, but I'm certain he wished he was with her."

"They have a special relationship that spans many years, and I've no doubt the duke has little reason to concern himself about who Lady Westcot drives with in the Park, no more than she need trouble herself over your presence in his carriage. It means nothing."

"One odd encounter was with Lord John. He was accompanied by the most beautiful creature imaginable, but His Grace ignored her and did not trouble to introduce her to me."

Mrs. Penrose laughed. "Oh my dear, naturally he would not. Lord John's high-flyer is bound to have been a cyprian. He is a considerable rake, you know."

Araminta felt foolish for not guessing. A line of carriages were waiting to let down their passengers, and at last the ladies in the Penrose coach were able to alight outside Barrington House, a splendid mansion of large proportions.

Sometime earlier, the guest of honor had arrived at his brother's house to be met by the strange sight of Greville Dunwoody pinning paper labels to the lapels of his twin sons' coats. On closer inspection, the duke saw that one bore a large letter A and the other a letter B.

"What the devil are you about?" the duke asked in some amusement. "A new fashion I know nothing about? Is there a label for each of us?"

Lord Dunwoody laughed. "It's a splendid lark, Avedon, and I owe the idea of it entirely to you."

The duke looked perplexed. "To me, Grev? What have I done to earn such acclaim?"

"It was something you remarked upon a while ago, Avedon. You made mention of the fact no one could tell the boys apart, so I thought it would be a lark to invite the guests to wager on whether twin A is Adolphus or Octavious."

A look of bewilderment and disbelief crossed the duke's face. "Grev, is your attic to let? You can't do such a thing!"

"Why not indeed? It's a novel wager, and that is what everyone is seeking."

"Novel indeed," the duke chided, still looking both irritated and amused, "but it still won't do."

The boys themselves then began to make noises of protest. "I am sorry, boys," their uncle apologized, "but it really will not do." He turned once again to his brother-in-law and explained, "Grev, there is no one to verify which twin is which."

"I know which one is which."

"*You* are not impartial," the duke pointed out, plucking the labels from their coats. "You need someone impartial to verify the outcome, otherwise you would be leaving yourself open to accusations of cheating from disgruntled losers."

Greville Dunwoody sighed and nodded. "I get your drift, Avedon. It was a crack-brained notion, I grant you."

The boys continued to voice their own protests as the duke said, " 'A' is Octavious. Correct?"

"No!" they chorused with much laughter joined by the duke and their father.

Lord John had just come down the stairs and was smiling blandly in the midst of all the hilarity. "It was only a little harmless fun, Avedon. Have you been so long ensconced in the country you've forgotten what a lark is about?"

The duke then drew his brother to one side and said in a low whisper so only he could hear, "Have you been self-indulgent for so long, John, you can no longer tell right from wrong?" The younger man looked mutinous as the duke went on, "I didn't take kindly to your attempt to embarrass me and Miss Penrose with your paramour."

Lord John then threw back his head and laughed. "Good grief, Avedon, you have become such a prosy old bore. You never used to be."

"On the contrary, Johnny, you remain just as ever you were, which is a great pity because I had hoped you'd learned some good sense."

His brother's smile faded, but any further angry exchanges were forestalled by the arrival of

Lady Betsey just as the first guests began to drift in.

"I do trust," Lord John said to his wife under his breath, "all is as it should be. As you insisted, my dear, I have left everything to you, and I hope I do not regret it."

Soon the rooms of the mansion filled with some of the highest-ranking, most influential and wealthiest people in the land. Although Lord John's dark eyes maintained a glittery look, he exhibited the famous Barrington charm as he greeted his guests, until he espied Lady Westcot arriving. He welcomed her effusively, but at the same time shot his wife a furious look as the countess cast a knowing one at the duke.

Her gown of magenta velvet was a perfect foil for her blond coloring, and no one was more aware than she of her allure.

"Diversions are distinctly more interesting when one knows you will be attending," she told the duke.

"How lovely you look, my lady," he greeted her before he turned briskly to her companion, Lord Belstone, who asked in a half whisper, "Is it true you've been secluded at Summerhills all these years surrounded by a bevy of fetching females?"

"You must come down and see for yourself" was the reply.

"So Belstone is her companion this evening," Lord John remarked as the couple made their way up the stairs to the ballroom. "I've heard that 'Ball' Hughes has bought her a splendid new carriage, and Prinny the team to go with it."

"She always did have countless admirers," the duke replied.

"There is an *on-dit* that reports that she has replaced Mrs. Jordan in the affections of the Duke of Clarence."

His brother looked amused. "What an old tattle-box you are becoming, Johnny. Do you eavesdrop on Betsey's tea parties?"

He noticed that Lady Betsey hid a smile behind her fan as her husband continued to look annoyed, but then Araminta arrived accompanied by her mother, and Lord John became angry again.

"I must bespeak a dance with you at the outset, Miss Penrose," the duke told her, "lest you be fully engaged later in the evening. I would not wish to miss the opportunity again."

Araminta's cheeks grew rather pink at his pointed reminder of their first encounter. Her gown of silver lace over white satin would have been fetching on someone with a finer figure and taller stance, but a quick glance around her proved she could not possibly shine in such elegant company. The duke himself looked quite splendid in his evening dress, his dark eyes smiling enigmatically into hers.

A quick retort came to her lips, but mindful of not displeasing him any more than she had already done, she curtsied and murmured, "I am most obliged to you for your condescension, Your Grace."

As she straightened up, she caught the eye of Lord John, who appeared to be less than pleased which was unusual, for he invariably put on a cheerful face in public. His wife, however, who invariably appeared terrified in company, was smiling slightly, and Araminta was startled, for there was something in the woman's demeanor that puzzled her. Lady Betsey was well known for her diffidence and lack of opinions, but just now it seemed there was more to her than was usual.

"So kind of you to invite us," Mrs. Penrose murmured.

"My wife has some difficulty in knowing where to stop," Lord John replied.

When the two Penrose ladies moved away, Lord John could contain his irritation no longer. "Betsey, I thought you told me you could manage the guest list on your own."

His wife's face was a picture of innocence as she replied, "I did, but what is amiss, dearest? Is there someone I missed out?"

He glanced uncomfortably at his brother before saying in a sibilant whisper, "You have invited all the wrong people. There are too many, especially those who would have designs upon my brother. Lady Westcot and that other young female of no consequence. Heaven knows why he wastes his time upon that little dab."

Lady Betsey continued to look dismayed. "Lady Westcot is a close friend of your sister, as is Miss Penrose's mother, dearest. I could not in all conscience omit their names for fear of offending Lady Dunwoody. You have always impressed upon me the importance of toadying to your sisters at every opportunity."

"Betsey dear," the duke broke in, aware that there was some discord between his brother and sister-in-law, "I hear the orchestra striking up, and we are engaged to lead the first set."

As he led her away, his brother continued to look

furious. He stared after the couple, and was further annoyed to note how happy Betsey looked while she conversed with the duke.

When she reached the top of the stairs, Lady Westcot had looked back at the duke, hoping to find him watching her, but all she saw was Araminta arriving with her mother, and her face took on a look of irritation.

"*Who* is that creature?" she demanded.

Lord Belstone looked blank. "I have no notion, my dear. Should I know who she is? She looks very ordinary, I confess."

"You're a ninnyhammer, Belstone. I saw her with Avedon in the Park the other day. She is not in the least his style and yet . . ."

Her companion smiled and assured her, "I don't believe Avedon is back in town to pay court to anyone, not even you, my dear."

Furiously she tapped him on the arm with her fan. "I did not solicit an opinion from you, Belstone, so be obliging enough to hold your tongue!"

As the duke led his sister-in-law into the set, he teased, "Betsey, I am beginning to believe you a schemer."

Once again Lady Betsey affected an air of innocence, and her cheeks took on a pinky hue. "I a schemer, Oliver? What a nonsense. Everyone knows me for what I am."

She laughed as he persisted. "Why, I wonder, was my brother so injured by the sight of two ladies of my acquaintance arriving here this evening?" When she made no reply, he added, "You seem intent upon putting them in my way."

"It would not be in my interest to do so."

"Exactly! However, it would certainly be against

Johnny's interest." Her cheeks became even more pink as he went on, "You would not be seeking a little gentle revenge upon him, would you, Betsey?"

"What kind of a wife would do such a thing?"

"One who is obliged to endure constant slights and occasional unkindnesses perhaps."

"You must consider me a wretch to think so."

"Far from it, my dear. Let people think what they wish, including your husband, and if they come to an incorrect conclusion, that is no fault of ours."

She smiled before she said, "You do have some purpose here, don't you?"

"Yes, but I'm afraid you might be a trifle disappointed when it is concluded."

"In that event, I must enjoy myself while I can."

"And I shall be obliged to dance carefully, once with each sister and never with any unmarried lady."

She gave him one of her rare laughs. "It must be devilishly hard being an eligible bachelor."

"Not nearly as difficult as being a husband, I fancy," he riposted as the set began.

EIGHT

More interest ensued when the duke came to claim Araminta for the promised dance. She was surprised at how nervous she was feeling at the prospect of standing up with him, for she knew they had not parted on the best of terms on the last occasion, and she had been quite certain it had ended any further connection between them. For someone more accustomed to the fawning of sycophants, it must be most vexing for him to find a female so resistant to his charm, and for once she wished she could be of a more placating nature.

"How kind of Lord John and Lady Betsey to invite us," she told him as he led her into the set.

He cast her an odd smile that she couldn't understand at all. "I believe Lady Betsey is entirely responsible for the guest list."

"She doesn't normally take as prominent a part as this in social events. In fact, I have never noticed her before."

Again the duke smiled oddly before he said in a careful tone, "She is one of those females who does not wish to be in the forefront of events, but be assured, she is up to all the rigs."

"I imagine she is obliged to be, married to Lord John."

Momentarily the duke's attention was diverted by Lady Betsey joining the set partnered by Sholto Farthington. He stared at them for a few moments before catching sight of Sir Leo Playfair, who smiled roguishly.

Turning back to Araminta, the duke asked in a casual tone, "Have you heard from Middlehampton of late?"

"I receive regular communications," she replied, her coolness returning.

"I trust that everything is well with Hal."

"As well as the situation allows, Your Grace."

The dance began, and the duke's choice of partner was observed by many who were intrigued, especially after their drive in the Park. Two people, also present that evening, were actively hostile to the pairing, innocent as it was. Lord John glowered at them from the edge of the dance floor, and Lady Westcot from her own place in the set, for she was never obliged to sit out a dance.

It was a great relief to her sometime later when the duke came to claim her for a cotillion, and she smiled, fluttering her fan at him in a flirtatious manner.

"I am of the opinion that you are neglecting me horribly, Avedon."

The duke's face took on a shocked expression. "I must beg your pardon if you consider I am doing so, my dear. If it is true, I must be the only gentleman in London who can stand so accused."

The look she gave him was a provocative one. "Just so, and I take it ill."

"I shall endeavor to remedy the situation as soon as my business in town is concluded."

109

"So business is the reason you have come to town so unexpectedly after all this time?"

"One of the reasons."

She gazed at him from beneath her long, dark lashes. "Is it at all possible you might have been prompted by a wish to become reacquainted with me?"

"My dear Lady Westcot, if I confess to such a thing, you are likely to become puffed up with your own consequence, and I don't wish to be responsible for that."

Lady Westcot's fan snapped shut, and her eyes flashed with anger. "You are already puffed up beyond your true consequence, Your Grace."

Fortunately, the music struck up and the dance began, observed by Araminta, who admired the well-matched pair from the edge of the dance floor. Lady Westcot's blond perfection was a foil to the duke's dark good looks. Drawing his own brooding attention from his brother, Lord John caught sight of Araminta watching them, and he went up to her, affecting his most ingratiating smile.

"Miss Penrose, is it not?"

Araminta was startled at being addressed by him for the first time. "Lord John?"

"Would you do me the honor of standing up for this set with me?"

The invitation startled her even further, for however discomforting the duke's company was to her, Lord John's was even worse, but she accepted. She was aware her drive with the duke had led to a certain amount of speculation among all those who did not know of their connection, but she did not feel it was in anyone's interest to explain. Now as she partnered his brother, who was a notorious

110

womanizer, she fervently hoped there would be no speculation about *them*.

Although Araminta was relieved when the dance was over, Lord John made no haste to leave her side, and as she was not engaged for the next set, she was obliged to converse with him for as long as he wished.

"I have been intrigued to observe your friendship with my brother, Miss Penrose."

She smiled and politely replied, "I assure you, it is scarcely that, my lord."

"As His Grace has been seen at various times in your company, I am sure you do yourself an injustice, dear."

Irritated by the inference, Araminta retorted, "It is only because I am acquainted with his ward, Henry Turlington. Our acquaintance stems only from that," she was at pains to point out, hoping this would end the gossip about her.

For a long moment, Lord John was quietly thoughtful as he digested the information, and then his face brightened to such a degree, he looked almost jubilant.

"I see now!" he breathed, and a moment later he inclined his head. "Your servant, ma'am," and was gone.

Araminta was slightly bewildered as he moved through the throng of people around the dance floor. So dense was the crowd, she could not see him approach Lady Westcot, who was in laughing conversation with a group of admirers.

He drew her aside after a few minutes, saying, "How do you enjoy our little soiree, my lady?"

"Tolerably well. It is, in fact, a far better diversion than I or many others expected it to be."

"So am I to assume many of my guests came only in hope of witnessing my wife make a mull of it?"

Lady Westcot's eyes sparkled. "I'm sure that isn't the only reason they have come, for who would have thought Lady Betsey could entertain so delightfully? You must be well pleased."

"Naturally, although I had no doubts about my wife's ability."

"You must ask her to do it again."

Lord John's face grew darker. "My wife and I are heartened to see you and my brother becoming re-acquainted after so many years apart."

"How kind of you to say so," she replied with a brittle laugh.

"After the hurt he caused you, you are generous in the extreme to extend to him the hand of friendship."

Lady Westcot's smile faded. "What do you mean by that?"

"When we were younger, I enjoyed Avedon's confidence much more than I do now, and I am aware it was he who gave you the go-by, although he was gallant enough to let everyone believe it was you who gave him his turnips."

She continued to look cross, and he added softly, "Don't get into a pucker over what I am saying, my lady. You can always rely upon my discretion, but I do counsel you to take care on this occasion. I would not wish your heart bruised yet again, and this time in the full glare of the public eye."

Her eyes narrowed. "What do you know, John Barrington?"

He smiled maddeningly before he answered, "A certain young lady—a surprising choice some will

112

say—is, I am afraid, very much in favor with my brother at present."

"Not that fubsy-faced milksop?" He nodded, and she inhaled through her teeth, tapping her fan thoughtfully against her palm. "I don't in the least understand what has happened to him."

"Confess that you never did."

"At one time Avedon would not have noticed a chit like that, even if he'd run her down in his carriage."

"Hardship has changed my brother out of all recognition, I fear."

"He appears little changed to me, except in that one respect."

"Miss Penrose is not in the least fetching, as you have observed, my lady, but she has a pleasing manner, and I don't suppose my brother will ever have cause to doubt her fidelity."

Lady Westcot cast him a furious look. "We shall see."

"Oh, no doubt," Lord John agreed in his silkiest manner.

"No man is ever leg-shackled until the preacher declares it to be so!"

So saying she flounced away from him and well pleased with his mischief making, he went to engage his wife in the next dance.

"Betsey, dear, you have done well tonight," he told her. "Everyone is singing your praises."

She cast him a suspicious look and then presumed, as was often the case, he had imbibed too freely of the champagne.

A little later, however, some of his bonhomie faded when he observed the duke laughing and flirting with Lady Westcot over supper. His little attempt at sabotage, it appeared, was not totally successful, but at least he could be satisfied that Miss Penrose was no danger to his position.

Araminta also observed the duke and Lady Westcot, and she felt unaccountably despondent. "Are you engaged for any of the dances after supper?" her mother asked anxiously.

"I regret I am not."

Mrs. Penrose smiled nonetheless. "There is yet time, and in any event you have, at least, stood up with the duke and Lord John."

"They don't really count, Mama," Araminta replied, her attention still centered upon the duke and his brother.

As the other guests began to drift back to the ballroom, she said, "I think I shall go and observe the gamesters in the card room, rather than be obliged to act the wallflower."

Mrs. Penrose looked at her in alarm. "Are you certain you only wish to observe the gaming?"

The girl smiled then, her face wrinkling into an expression of mischief. "Does it matter if I indulge a little, Mama?"

Bella Penrose lowered her voice to a whisper. "Araminta, this is not Middlehampton. Here you are surrounded by expert gamesters, my dear. No one plays for chicken stakes at these functions."

"I am fully aware of it, Mama, but I have suddenly lost all heart for social matters," she replied, before wandering away in the direction of the card room.

All the tables were already full, and many of the guests surrounded them, watching the play, occasionally commenting and frequently cheering on those who might be better served observing a little more reserve. When a chair became available, vacated by an early loser, Araminta hesitated only briefly before she sat down, smiling shyly at the other gamesters. The three gentlemen already seated at the table looked at her in surprise.

"My dear," Lord Belstone told her in what she was quick to recognize as a most patronizing manner, "this table is not for rank beginners."

"At home I play often, so I do not consider myself a beginner, my lord." He smiled at her indulgently as she confided in a diffident way, "I have a little pin money by me and will play only until it has gone. A game or two only."

The three gentlemen exchanged knowing looks, and then Lord Belstone told her, "It will be a pleasure to game with such a fetching opponent, ma'am."

When the duke strolled into the card room sometime later, he was first of all surprised to see Araminta Penrose gambling with three of the most expert gamesters of the ton. His surprise grew even greater when he approached the table and saw the amount of money she had accumulated, for it was certain she could not have brought so large an amount with her.

Humbert Crossley-King got up, threw down his cards angrily, and bowing, he strode away from the table. Araminta looked alarmed when the duke replaced him at the table.

"Dame Fortune certainly favors you this evening," he remarked, causing her cheeks to redden.

"Devilishly good gamester, Miss Penrose," Lord Belstone admitted. "And she has youth on her side. Crossley-King didn't like being bested by a female."

"None of us do," the duke replied amiably, before he turned to look directly at Araminta, who began to gather up her modest winnings. "Mama will be furious with me," she murmured.

"She will be delighted to see you've won," the duke told her. Then, frowning, he added, "Surely you are going to be sporting enough to allow these gentlemen an opportunity to win back their money."

" 'Tis only a trifle," Lord Belstone explained.

"Not to me," Araminta said under her breath.

Before she could escape, the duke began to deal the cards. "I do hope you are not running away on my account, Miss Penrose," he said smoothly.

She froze. Her gaze met his steely one across the table. She knew a challenge when she heard one and sank back into the chair, her lips compressed into a stubborn line. There seemed to be some special atmosphere about that table that attracted more observers, or perhaps, she mused, it was the sight of the Duke of Avedon back gaming after years of enforced abstinence, moreover pitting his wits against those of a green girl. All of the other debutantes were happier seeking partners for dancing in the ballroom, and would no doubt shrink back in horror at the very thought of risking one guinea in play against any of these practiced gamesters.

After her initial and rather heady flush of success, Araminta watched in dismay her winnings dwindle, as his steadily accumulated. Clearly, he was the best gamester she had ever encountered. Her previous success in the drawing rooms of Middlehampton was of no account now.

She stared at the dwindling pile of coins in front

of her, before she glanced across at the duke who was watching her, amusement evident in his eyes. He wanted her to withdraw! she realized. To capitulate! The alternative was public humiliation.

Araminta cast him a defiant look before she said in clipped tones, "Be pleased to deal, Your Grace."

One or two observers gasped as the duke did so. There was a murmuring, too, when to her great relief, she won the next game. Excitement was palpable in that part of the room when she won again. More people drifted over to watch as her winnings began to accumulate once again. Her head began to swim as the necessary cards were never available to the duke. She was scarcely aware of the excited murmurings all around at this point. Common sense urged her to stop while she was ahead, but Araminta could not. Excitement drove her on, that and the sure knowledge that this was not likely to happen again.

At last, the duke declared, "You've brought me to buckle and thong, Miss Penrose. I'm all dished up for one evening."

She stared in astonishment at her winnings, and then at the duke. He did not appear in the least annoyed at losing. He appeared to be taking his losses in very good part, no doubt because what was a large amount of money to her represented a mere bagatelle to him.

His gaze was steady, amused even, and then the awful truth dawned on her. He had allowed her to win. For whatever warped reason, he had chosen to dish himself.

Araminta jumped to her feet, pushing back the chair as she did so. Fury tore at her, although few would have guessed as she stared across at the loser. She was tempted to toss her winnings at him, but prudence held her back. There was far more at stake than hurt pride, and she quickly gathered the winnings into her bulging reticule and went out to find her mother.

Sometime later, the duke strolled back to the ballroom, but was unable to locate either Araminta or her mother.

However, his brother quickly sidled up to him, murmuring slyly, "The little bird has flown, Avedon." The duke cast him a cold look. "It is one way of providing oneself with means, although for a debutante, it is a trifle unusual. However, I am persuaded, you are man enough not to be grieved at being trounced by a green girl just out of the schoolroom. Quite a surprising filly, is our Miss Penrose in many ways."

Before the duke could deliver a cutting reply, Lady Westcot glided up to him. Turning her back pointedly on Lord John, she addressed the duke. "I fear the strain of poor Westcot's demise is still affecting me, and I feel quite faint. Would you be kind enough to escort me home, Avedon?"

"Did you not arrive with Belstone?" Lord John asked.

"Belstone will stay at the gaming tables until dawn," she retorted.

"How can I possibly refuse a lady in distress?" the duke responded, much to his brother's further annoyance.

As he escorted her away, Lady Westcot glanced back to smile wickedly at the scowling Lord John. As she and the duke came down the stairs, Araminta and her mother were just about to leave, and the sight of the duke in a carefree conversation with

Lady Westcot, with whom it was evident he was about to depart, did nothing to assuage her anger toward him.

"I cannot help but feel rather strongly that Lord John has taken me in dislike, although I cannot conceive why," Lady Westcot was saying in a piteous voice.

The duke transferred his attention back to her immediately. "You must not for a moment think so, my dear. It is no personal reflection upon you, who is so very well loved by all who know you." She dimpled and he went on, "Johnny dislikes *any* female in whose company I find myself, which augurs badly for most females of the ton!"

119

NINE

"A concert of ancient music!" the duke cried. "I cannot conceive of that, Timmins. Tell me you are roasting me."

The groom stood in the center of the study, looking abashed. "I assure you it's true, Your Grace. I couldn't find a maidservant willing to strike up a conversation, however much I hung around Berkeley Street, just an old squeeze-crab who used to be Miss Penrose's nursemaid. Then Dottie, Lady Nayler's servant girl, caught me and cut up stiff. She'll be riding rusty all week now, Your Grace."

"Yes, yes, Timmins," the duke said testily, "spare me the details of your sordid private life. Just tell me all you have learned about Miss Penrose."

"That evening you were at Lord John's house in Grosvenor Square, Your Grace, I made it my business to strike up a conversation with the coachman of the Penrose carriage."

"Good thinking, Timmins."

"Thank you, Your Grace. The old cat at the Penrose house wouldn't give me the time o' day."

"And?" the duke inquired, cutting short what might have gone on to be a diatribe against Miss Penrose's maidservant.

"I began to grumble—pretending like—about all the places I'm obliged to go for my master, and the fellow obligingly blew the gaff. Fulsome he was and no mistake. He told me that his people enjoyed concerts of ancient music at the Hanover Square Rooms and have another one to go to next Thursday. Very cultured his people are, he tells me. They've been to every museum and gallery in the city since they arrived. Miss Penrose says, apparently, they might never have the opportunity again and needs must make the most of their stay."

"She would," groaned the duke. "It seems the worst Miss Penrose can do to my ward is bore him to death, and yet . . ." He looked up at the groom. "You say they will attend a concert this Thursday?"

"Yes, Your Grace, Grice, for that's the fellow's name, is sure of it."

"Do you think you can find out any more from him, Timmins?"

"I've arranged to meet him for a friendly noggin or two at the Duck and Plover, Your Grace."

The duke smiled and then brought a coin out of his waistcoat pocket, which he handed to the groom. "Make certain Mr. Grice is afforded plenty of hospitality, Timmins."

The fellow grinned. "Rely on me, Your Grace, and it shall be done." As he was just bowing himself out of the room, he paused to add, "Grice also told me that Miss Penrose keeps pestering him to take her to St. Bartholomew's Fair, Your Grace, but he refuses, naturally."

The duke frowned. "Why the devil does she want to go there, I wonder?"

"She declares it would be diverting."

121

"There could scarcely be a greater difference than between concerts of ancient music and the goings on at St. Bartholomew's Fair."

"Grice tells me that Miss Penrose is a most singular young lady, much given to unconventional whims."

The duke smiled then and found himself suddenly approving. "Mayhap Miss Penrose will have her wish."

"That's no place for a lady of Quality," Timmins pointed out, looking doubtful.

"Not for some ladies of Quality, in any event," the duke replied with a laugh before dismissing the groom at last.

As the mantel clock chimed the hour, he sat down to pen a note, which he then handed to a footman for delivery to Lady Westcot. When he had finished he took out his gold hunter and checked the time before calling for his curricle to be brought around.

"Oh, the humiliation of it!" Araminta lamented, much to her mother's dismay.

"Surely you cannot still be moaning about your remarkable piece of good fortune, Minty," Mrs. Penrose chided. "You have never done so before."

"That is exactly the point. On this occasion, it was not good fortune, not in the least. It was my *mis*fortune ever to meet that man. Hal never once intimated he was actually so wicked, but now I see that he is."

"Minty, dear, if it is true he allowed you to win, and with your skill, it is by no means certain, then surely it was out of some misguided kindness on His Grace's part."

"He has no notion of kindness, Mama. If he had,

he would have given permission for the wedding to take place without this unwarranted delay. It amused him to let me win, knowing I could say nothing for fear of causing a scandal. I daresay, he would have relished *that*!"

Bella Penrose shook her head. "Such a large amount, though, Minty. I cannot believe he would be so crack-brained to lose it deliberately just to amuse himself."

"To us it is a large amount of money, Mama, but to the Duke of Avedon, it is almost a nothing."

"If you are so incensed at what you perceive an injustice, why do you not return all your winnings to him?"

"It would be just another opportunity for him to humiliate us. I can just see the ironic expression on his face, hear the clever, cutting remarks he would make. It would be a gift to him that I am unwilling to bestow."

"I cannot imagine His Grace being so devious, dearest, really I can't."

"You have a blinkered opinion of him, Mama, much as it regrets me to say so, and it is just like so many other females. I see him as the manipulative creature he really is. He is aggrieved, don't you see, that I don't beg him to relent. That is what he truly wishes."

Mrs. Penrose looked thoughtful. "I believe I have allowed this matter to dominate your time in London to a far greater degree than I should. I should have had words with His Grace at the outset, and I don't believe it to be too late even now."

Araminta looked horrified. "No, Mama, I beg of you not to go. We must, if nothing else, retain our pride."

"What does pride matter if you are so dreadfully unhappy?"

"The matter will eventually be resolved without recourse to such embarrassing ploys. In the meantime, Mama," she added, her ill humor entirely gone, "I am going to put my winnings to good use."

"How can you do so, dearest?" her mother asked, wide-eyed.

"Just assure me that you will not approach His Grace about the other matter."

"If you do not wish me to approach him, I won't, only I cannot bear to see you made so unhappy."

"I shall endeavor not to let it tease me any further, only the injustice of it angers me so." Her mother looked considerably relieved as Araminta tapped her copy of the *Ladies' Monthly Museum.* "You and I are going to Layton and Shear in Henrietta Street to choose some materials for new gowns, and then we will take our purchases to Mademoiselle Roquette for making up into the latest French fashions, all courtesy of His Grace the Duke of Avedon!"

Mrs. Penrose's face flushed with pleasure. "Is that not a trifle too extravagant, dearest?"

Araminta was already hurrying toward the door, but she paused before she opened it. "Extravagant? Of course not, Mama. It shouldn't only be peacocks that have the finest plumes!"

TEN

"If only I possessed blue eyes, so that their color was enhanced by that of the bonnet," Araminta lamented as she gazed at her reflection in the pier glass.

Her latest purchase, a bonnet with a huge poke brim lined with ruched satin and tied with a matching satin bow at her cheek, was the most stylish she had ever possessed. Even so, she was aware it required a startling beauty to do it real justice.

"It looks fine enough to me, Miss Minty," the maidservant declared. "A little fancy perhaps."

"It is fine enough, only I am not."

"What a nonsense," the woman chided. "You're as fine a looking young lady as any, and no mistake."

"Nothing about me is quite *right*, and although that has never troubled me before, I cannot help but wish that I was beautiful, Mary, for beauties can achieve so much."

"Those who care for you, do so for yourself," the maidservant told her. "You'd do well to remember that."

"Oh, I do, but it is evident if I was a little more fetching, I might resolve this teasing problem swiftly. Don't you see?"

The maidservant stared at her mistress uncomprehendingly. "No, ma'am, I can't say that I do."

Araminta smiled wryly and turned to the woman at last. "Very well, Mary. Fetch your hat and pelisse, and we will go out. On your way, take the letter lying on the dresser and see it is dispatched for me." As Mary picked up the missive, she glanced at the address and sniffed loudly. "Mama is resting, so I may as well take the opportunity to call upon Miss Webber and mayhap impress her with my new finery."

"Shall I send for the coachman, ma'am?"

"Miss Webber's house is only a short distance away, and it's a fine day. We shall walk and mayhap draw a good deal of attention on the way."

The duke drove around the corner of Piccadilly and into Berkeley Street with great precision, the team of horses under his whip acting as one. He had not seen Araminta Penrose since the evening at his brother's house, nor had he received any further communication from his ward, and all at once he felt uneasy, although he could not understand why.

Although he had been unable to unearth anything untoward about the Penrose family, it seemed there was more to Miss Penrose than was initially thought. His lawyer had made a brief investigation on the duke's behalf and had declared them perfectly respectable, if a mite impoverished, which was only what he knew already. However, Miss Penrose was beginning to intrigue him a great deal. Her skill at the cards was considerable, even if it was not as great as his own. He was suddenly aware there might be other qualities, both good and bad, about Hal's beloved that remained to be discovered.

As his curricle moved along the road, he suddenly drew on the ribbons, bringing it to an abrupt stop.

"Miss Penrose?" he called.

Araminta, who had been walking along, not noting any of the carriages passing by, started at the sound of her name. As she looked up at him from beneath the brim of her new bonnet, she was shocked at the unexpected encounter and hoped that fact wasn't too evident to him. She was sure he would immediately guess why she was dressed in so splendid a manner. Her pelisse was also new. It was made from the finest French velvet and frogged extravagantly with gold braid.

"Your Grace," she gasped, drawing back a little in alarm, and then her face took on a resolute look as she recalled their last encounter over a pack of cards.

"How fortunate I should encounter you."

"I don't see why you should feel in the least like that, Your Grace. The last time we met, it cost you dear."

"Oh, I shall not quickly engage you in gaming again, Miss Penrose. My pockets are to let."

She cast him a disbelieving look as he added, "I was on my way to my sister's house."

"Does not Lady Dunwoody live in the other direction?"

He continued to smile. "My sister, Lady Stanyon, lives in this direction. May I offer you a ride to wherever you are going?"

"No, I thank you," she answered firmly, retaining her unforgiving stance. "My destination is but a short way."

Somewhat to her alarm, he handed the ribbons

127

to his tiger and climbed down to join her at the curbside. His height increased by his tall beaver hat seemed to overwhelm her. "Truth to tell, Miss Penrose, I am a little lost this afternoon. I shall in all probability find my sister out. I had originally thought to visit St. Bartholomew's Fair, but doubted it would be diverting on my own." He noted the spark of interest in her expression, and he went on, "I don't suppose you would take pity upon a fellow newcomer to town and accompany me there?"

"You are scarcely considered a newcomer, Your Grace. I fancy you will have more invitations than you can possibly accept."

"Certainly more than I care to accept, that is true. During my stay in the country, I have come to enjoy more rustic pastimes, and I feel you might be of a similar mind."

She met his level gaze. "I confess, I have long wished to visit the fair myself, but as yet have not contrived to engage anyone kind enough to accompany me."

The duke looked shocked. "Surely not, Miss Penrose."

Ignoring what appeared to be sarcasm in his manner, she said, "It is most vexing to me, for in Middlehampton I am allowed to visit the poor and the sick, and enjoy all our country fairs. Here in London, I am informed such places are out of bounds for a lady."

"I would agree that going alone would be most foolhardy for a female of gentle birth. However, if you wish to accompany me, then you need have no qualms, and I would be most grateful for the company."

Araminta's face took on an expression of stubbornness. "I do think, Your Grace, in view of a certain difference of opinion between us, it would not be advisable for us to be in one another's company more often than is necessary."

"Balderdash, Miss Penrose!" was the duke's unequivocal reply. "I hadn't considered you to be so hen-hearted."

"Hen-hearted? Does one have to be brave to endure your company, Your Grace?"

He laughed disarmingly. "It has often been said of me," he admitted, "but I believe you are up to the challenge, ma'am."

Much of her resentment faded at that moment, and she ventured, "If I do agree to accompany you, may I drive the curricle?"

If his invitation was meant to be some kind of challenge, Araminta did not see why she should not issue a challenge of her own.

He laughed. "Miss Penrose, this is no governess cart."

"If it were, I would not wish to tool the ribbons."

"The team is a fast one, the traffic we are like to encounter daunting."

"I assure you such difficulties won't be any problem to me."

In the face of her implacable certainty and the challenging look she shot him, he said a moment later, "Oh, very well, but I hope I do not regret this."

Araminta smiled wryly as she dismissed her most unwilling maidservant and then allowed him to help her onto the box. As he did, so the duke glanced back at the surly maid, assuming that this was the uncooperative creature Timmins had encountered. As she climbed up, Araminta had noted that the tiger looked disapproving, too, but once the duke had joined her on the box, ribbons in hand, she set the team in motion.

"I must tell you, I have wanted to do this ever since I saw your chariot," she declared, her eyes bright.

"I wish you had told me that afternoon in the Park, for it would have been much better for you to drive there."

"Fustian!" she retorted. "That cannot be termed driving, at such a snail's pace."

His eyebrows rose a little in surprise before he admitted, "So far you are handling the team well."

"Why should I not? I have driven Mr. Turlington's curricle, although I own it is not as fine or as fashionable as yours."

"Turn right here. There is considerable building going on, which causes much congestion. I am told that His Royal Highness has commissioned the building of a splendid new thoroughfare called New Street."

"I imagine that when it is completed it will become known as Regent Street. His Royal Highness is adept at naming places after himself."

The duke looked amused. "You seem to disapprove of that."

"On the contrary. I would love to have a street named after me."

He continued to look amused as she maneuvered the curricle in and out of the traffic. "Araminta Street has a certain ring to it, I confess. You are driving very well indeed, Miss Penrose. You have many hidden talents."

Araminta interrupted her concentration to steal

a glance at him. "They are not in the least remarked upon in a gentleman. Moreover, it is most vexing when a female endowed with great beauty is not expected to possess any further qualities, whereas a female who is positively plain is required to be stupid, too!"

"I hope you do not refer to yourself, for plainspoken you may be, but plain you most definitely are not!"

She caught her breath and turned to look at him in amazement, only for him to reach out to grab the ribbons to avoid a collision with a loaded cart. The area they were now traveling through was far from the elegant squares and terraces of Mayfair, and she readily understood why it would be foolhardy for ladies to travel here on their own.

"Oh dear," she wailed as the carter shook his fist in her direction. "I almost caused your paint work to be scratched!"

"To the devil with the paint work! How would I have explained your cracked skull to your mother?"

She began to laugh as the spire of St. Bartholomew's Church came into sight, and she marveled at how easily he was able to disarm her. She had entirely forgotten her resentment over their card game.

Here the traffic began to be thicker, and pedestrians making their way to the fair were strewn all over the road. The duke took charge of the curricle again, and Araminta looked at him in dismay.

"Must you? I was just growing used to your team."

"Yes, I'm afraid I must, Miss Penrose," he retorted, "lest a pleasant drive becomes a total fiasco."

"It was a most invigorating ride."

"For me, too," he answered dryly and then, casting her a glance, he added, "I might well allow you to tool the ribbons again."

"You are being exceedingly indulgent of me of late, Your Grace. It is quite flattering."

"The intention was not to flatter you, Miss Penrose. I just don't want you to think me too unobliging, or at least unobliging in everything."

When he glanced at her again, he saw she was staring down at her gloved hands and he said abruptly, as he brought the curricle to a halt, "We shall be obliged to walk from here."

All approaches to the area around St. Bartholomew's Church were blocked with carts, carriages, barrows, and boxes as well as crowds of people and animals. The duke left the curricle in the charge of his tiger, and after handing Araminta down, he kept a firm hold of her arm as they walked toward the fair, accosted at every step by peddlers.

He noted that her eyes shone with excitement as she looked around. "We have nothing like this at Middlehampton, just a hiring fair and a May fair."

"It's much the same in Sussex, although I daresay it is diverting enough. My workers and tenants appear to enjoy the rustic simplicity of such fairs."

"They don't have your access to more sophisticated entertainments."

"I do appreciate that fact, Miss Penrose, and I am bound to say that you appear to be enjoying this far more than any ton party."

"That is so true!" she admitted with a laugh. "I am not in the least *tonnish*."

"From all I have observed, you appear to fit in easily in such circles."

"I am naturally making the most of my time in London."

"Are you always so pragmatic?"

"I suppose I must be, although I confess Papa declared it was a waste of good money to launch me, but Mama insisted that I have a Season. Poor Mama has her dreams, but I made it clear to her, I would not find a husband in London. I did not wish to." Suddenly her cheeks flushed with color. "I do beg your pardon, Your Grace. I should not have spoken so candidly."

"If only more people would," he replied. "I understand that Mr. Penrose has remained in Middlehampton."

Araminta laughed. "Papa loathes cities. He finds it an ordeal to go into Middlehampton when it is necessary for him to do so. He is far happier at home."

"That, I fancy, is also true of *you*."

The streets around St. Bartholomew's Church were lined with stalls selling various foodstuffs, oysters, whelks, gingerbread, and sweetmeats. All the vendors called out their wares, creating a marvelous cacophony of noise that attracted Araminta's attention most welcomingly just then.

"Would you like some gingerbread?" the duke asked.

"No, I thank you, but I do adore sugarplums."

The delighted vendor pocketed the duke's proferred coin, and Araminta accepted the bag of sugarplums, eating one each as they moved on.

"Mama will be mortified to know I am here," she declared a moment later.

"Even if she knows you are with me?"

Araminta looked all at once shy. "She will at least be happy to know I am safe in your company."

"That means she cannot hold me in as much dislike as you, Miss Penrose."

Araminta stopped in her tracks and turned to face him. "Dislike? Be assured I do not dislike you, Your Grace. In fact, I like you exceedingly well. If I were a gentleman, I should aspire to be just like you—at least in most respects."

His eyes were wide with surprise. "I thank you kindly, ma'am."

"I just disagree with you in one matter over which you have complete control, and that I consider most unfair."

"Your loyalty to those you are for is commendable."

She began to walk on, and he followed close behind. "Loyalty to our loved ones is essential, don't you think, Your Grace?"

For a moment, he appeared to be considering the question before he replied, "That, and responsibility, of course."

"That word is a blanket for all manner of abuses," she retorted. They had come to a halt outside one of the booths. "Like this," she added, although she couldn't help but chuckle.

The booth bore the name of Dr. Van Cheatall, who was espousing his curative medicine to the interest of the crowd that had gathered to hear him.

"There you are, Miss Penrose," the duke pointed out, "the cure for everything that ails you."

"I shall certainly purchase a bottle, even though I'm persuaded it cannot possibly cure my megrims." She looked up at him from beneath the brim of her bonnet. "Only you can do that."

"Try this instead," he suggested, guiding her quickly toward the Merry Andrew, whose antics soon had her laughing.

The duke viewed her enjoyment with indulgence, and when the sound of drums and trumpets arrested them, he guided her toward a platform where actors were parading to advertise a performance of *The Wandering Outlaw*.

"I wonder if a performance is about to begin," she murmured, unable to hide her excitement.

"I imagine that is why they are here."

"How wonderful it must be to be a thespian," Araminta enthused as she watched them parade with bright eyes.

"I am told it is a hard life."

"But less constricting than being a lady or a gentleman."

Once again he looked surprised. "You sound as if you'd prefer it."

"Indeed I would!" Then she looked abashed. "I believe I am too fond of my creature comforts to enjoy such an itinerate life."

"Would you like to go inside?" he asked as the barker called out the entertainment to be enjoyed within the booth.

"Oh yes, indeed," she replied, needing no more encouragement.

He paid the entrance fee, and they passed into the booth. Araminta settled down on the rackety bench and declared, "We have visited all the fashionable theaters in London, but nothing is quite as exciting as this!"

"It is certainly unusual," he agreed, removing his high-crowned beaver and glancing about him.

He was surprised to find her enjoying such simple

entertainments. Only the poorest people, who could not afford the theater, came to fairs and watched such basic entertainment. He never thought to find a debutante who would be diverted by a fair, and he was somewhat moved by her pleasure.

As soon as the booth was filled, and Araminta seemed unaffected by the unappetizing aroma of those in close proximity to her, the entertainment began. She watched the unfolding story in fascination and then, in the last scene, where the avenging ghost appears, unconsciously she clung onto the duke's arm. He moved closer to her and patted her arm reassuringly. By comparison he found the unsophisticated proceedings not in the least diverting, but he was amused by her reaction, and he watched her with great pleasure. The expression on her face changed constantly with the action taking place, and he was amazed that he had ever considered her plain.

The moment the melodrama ended, Araminta became aware of how close to the duke she was sitting. She became immediately self-conscious and drew away in much confusion. Everyone in the booth was obliged to sit close together, but all at once it was a little too close for her comfort.

A comic harlequinade followed, which amused the audience, and although Araminta laughed, she continued to feel embarrassed and aware of his closeness as never before.

When they emerged sometime later into the light of day, she blinked, saying, "I cannot recall when I have enjoyed myself more, certainly not since I came to London."

"That is true for me, too," he affirmed, and she looked at him in disbelief. Quickly he went on, "I regret, though, we must start back, else Mrs. Penrose might send a Runner in pursuit of us."

Silent now, she walked at his side experiencing an odd feeling of sadness that she could not understand. They spent a while on the way inspecting the exotic animals in Wombwell's Menagerie, paused to watch a dwarf dressed in a sailor's uniform dancing a hornpipe, and decided between them that the hairy creature known as the man-monkey looked like neither man nor monkey.

The curricle awaited them where they had left it, but as they made their way toward it, Araminta's attention was attracted by an altercation taking place at the side of the road. A few people were watching with interest, some in amusement. Then she gasped in annoyance when she saw that all the interest was concentrated on some wretched fellow who was beating his less than willing horse who, she noted quickly, appeared more than a little undernourished.

The duke glanced across at the fracas with little interest and was about to comment upon it when Araminta left his side to march across the road, her features set into an angry mask as she pushed her way through the assembled crowd.

"Miss Penrose . . . !" the duke called, starting after her.

She did not heed him, if indeed she had heard. "Stop it!" she cried as the frightened creature reared up, earning the further wrath of his master. "Stop it this instant I say!"

"Miss Penrose," the duke cried once again as he pushed his way forward. "This is none of your concern."

By way of a reply, she reached out to grab the

man's raised hand to prevent his whip from striking the horse again. The man rounded on her furiously, and she stepped back.

" 'Ere, what's the jib?" he roared.

"I demand that you stop beating this poor creature," Araminta told him breathlessly, her own anger tempered by fear.

" 'Es a lazy good for nothin', that's what 'e is."

One or two observers agreed.

The duke stood by looking amused, but for once Araminta was not aware of him. "How can you expect him to work? He's starving as well as frightened."

"Well, I beg your pardon, miss," the man said with heavy sarcasm. "I'll just go and get 'im a cushion to rest 'is 'ead."

Araminta drew in a sharp breath as watched by the amused onlookers he began to struggle and beat the unfortunate animal again. "Are you going to let him do this?" she asked the duke, who replied, "You can't make a good master out of a bad one."

"I've got to show 'im who's the master 'ere," the fellow retorted. "Not that much different to a woman. Right, guv'nor?"

He winked at the duke, who snapped, "Watch your tongue, or you'll be at the receiving end of some Turkish treatment yourself."

The man turned away and attempted to drag the unwilling horse along by a piece of rope. "All 'es good for is the knackers yard, and that's just where 'es going."

Exasperated, Araminta cried, "You can't do that!"

"Who's goin' to stop me?"

"How much will you get for him? I'll give you five guineas."

The duke put a restraining hand on her arm. "Miss Penrose, I beg of you . . ."

"Ten guineas!" she said in desperation.

The crowd gasped. The owner turned, pushed his greasy hat to the back of his head, and then thrust the end of the rope toward her. "Ten, you say?"

"Yes," Araminta replied, glancing uneasily at the duke who quickly added, "The lady is a great funster."

"A deal's a deal," the man insisted.

"Indeed," Araminta assured him, opening her reticule and counting out the coins.

As she did so, she ignored the cluck of the duke's tongue. As soon as she had counted out the last coin, the satisfied vendor moved away.

Clutching the horse's rope, Araminta at last raised her eyes to meet those of her companion. "I could not allow him to continue ill-treating this poor creature," she said lamely.

The horse whinnied, as if in agreement with her, and the duke eyed him in disgust. "I am bound to say, I believe you could have spent your money more wisely, Miss Penrose."

Her eyes flashed with defiance. "I cannot agree with you on that point, Your Grace."

"It is evident to me that this creature is burnt to the socket and is not long for the world. In fact, I must warn you, he appears about to drop his leaf."

"Stuff and nonsense! He needs only feeding and a little care and attention, that is all."

"Where do you intend to care for him?" he inquired politely.

For a moment, Araminta looked confounded, then she said, "I shall pay for him to be stabled."

"Good stabling is expensive."

She bit her lip. "I shall contrive," she told him, staring at him defiantly.

The duke took the rope from her, and the horse whinnied nervously, stepping back. "He's terrified," she said, and much to his discomfiture, two tears spilled onto her cheeks.

Suddenly angry, His Grace began to lead the horse toward the curricle. "I daresay some room may be found in a corner of my own stables."

Her demeanor brightened immediately, and Araminta skipped after him. "Oh, how wonderful of you to offer, Your Grace! I had no notion you were so good! I shall write to Hal and tell him of your offer."

"You will do no such thing."

"Why don't you wish people to think well of you?" she asked in some perplexity.

"They already do. I just don't wish anyone to think my attic's to let."

"I am more than willing to pay for his keep."

"Naturally." He paused to glance at her. "Shall I bill you weekly or monthly?"

Unsure whether he was gammoning her or not, Araminta replied, "Whatever pleases you, Your Grace. Dobbin and I will be eternally grateful to you."

The duke had been tying the creature to the back of his curricle, and when he straightened up, he was frowning, "Dobbin, Miss Penrose?"

Her cheeks grew red. "That is the name I have given him."

The tiger looked aghast at the scraggy horse being attached to the splendid, shiny curricle and exclaimed, "Your Grace . . . !"

Turning on his heel, the duke snapped, "Not a

word!" and the fellow became silent, but continued to look disapproving.

Araminta patted the miserable horse before allowing the duke to hand her up. "I really am most obliged to you," she told him as she sat down on the box.

"I would be very much obliged to *you*, Miss Penrose, if you would not tell anyone about this little incident."

She looked amused as he climbed onto the box next to her and took up the ribbons. "You evidently prefer people to consider you hard-hearted, but you are not—at least not where animals are concerned."

At his frowning look, she fell silent, but she continued to smile nevertheless. During the drive back to Berkeley Street, she made no attempt to engage him in conversation. On this occasion, she had made no attempt to persuade him to allow her to drive. She just glanced back occasionally at the now placid creature, trotting behind the curricle.

After a while, she became deeply pensive, and only when the curricle came to a stop outside number sixty-five did she start out of her reverie, amazed that they had arrived back so quickly.

The duke jumped down and offered her a helping hand. When Araminta stepped from the curricle, she was at a loss for words, averting her eyes from his shyly.

"Thank you for taking me to the fair. It has long been my wish to go."

"It has been a most unusual afternoon for me, too," he assured her. She stole a glance at him at last, looking for any signs of insincerity, but what she did see caused the blood to rise into her cheeks. "Nor need you make any further mention of that

141

miserable creature tied to the back of my curricle. I only hope no one of my acquaintance sees him before he is safely deposited in my stables."

Her lips quirked into a smile, and then she looked away again, but before she could make her escape, he took both her hands in his and raised them briefly to his lips, smiling into her eyes all the while before releasing them at last. Araminta paused long enough to pat Dobbin and entreat him to be good, and then she hurried into the house before the duke could realize she was trembling.

No sooner did she step over the threshold than her mother came hurrying into the hall, looking concerned. Araminta, who was still clutching her bag of sugarplums, untied her bonnet ribbons with hands that were still trembling.

"Minty, Mary said you had gone off with the Duke of Avedon. Is that so?"

Araminta could not just then meet her mother's eyes, but she nodded. "We met by chance in the street, and we went for a drive."

"A drive! Again! Why, Minty, this is most significant. Don't you agree?"

The young lady managed to nod yet again as she walked blindly toward the stairs, assailed by the oddest feelings she knew she must be alone to evaluate.

ELEVEN

"Before we return home, I just wish to call in at Floris in Jermyn Street," Araminta told her maid, who sat huddled in a cloak at the other side of the rather shabby Penrose carriage.

"As you wish, Miss Minty," the woman replied, "but that house will never seem like home to me."

"I have been told Floris sells the finest rose-scented soap in London, and I still have a little of my winnings left. Mama will enjoy a little gift like that, I fancy."

"I don't approve of gaming, Miss Minty, as well you know."

Araminta's eyes sparkled with mischief. "I have it in mind, Mary, you do not approve of London in general."

The maidservant's lips compressed in a disapproving line. "Can't say that I do, Miss Minty. Downright dangerous, it is."

One of Araminta's eyebrows rose slightly. "Indeed? I have to confess, I haven't yet found it to be particularly dangerous, aside from my brief encounter with that dreadful man who beat Dobbin, and I cannot truly regard it as such."

"Step out of the house, and you're likely to be knocked down by some young spark in a fancy carriage, and if not, sent senseless by a peddler's cart. Oh no, Miss Minty, you give me the peace of Middlehampton anytime."

Araminta laughed. "What an alarming picture you paint, Mary. I intend to watch my step very carefully from now on."

"We should never have come, and I said so to Cook. Leaving poor Mr. Penrose with only that goosecap Celia to tend him. It isn't right, and you taken away from all who love you and thrust into the company of strangers who don't care a jot. Criminal, I call it."

Some of Araminta's amusement faded, and she lapsed into an uncomfortable reverie until the carriage drew up outside the renowned perfumery. Since her outing to the fair with the duke, Araminta had found her thoughts returning to it time and time again, something that had nothing to do with her rescue of the horse. She reminisced at every odd moment about what he had said to her and how he had looked, in a way that was all too ominous for her peace of mind.

"Don't fret, Mary," she assured the woman as the footman put down the steps, "we'll be returning to Middlehampton before too long, but I shall never regret my time here."

"It won't be soon enough for me," the maidservant muttered.

Just as Araminta was going into the shop, a figure hurried out past her. She paid no attention to her until someone called her name, and Araminta turned, realizing it was Lady Betsey Barrington she had passed.

"Miss Penrose, is it not?" Lady Betsey asked.

"Why yes, ma'am. How nice to see you again. Your soiree was most enjoyable."

The woman smiled, toying nervously with the small package in her hand. "It is kind of you to say so. We always seem to meet when there are others around or at inopportune moments such as this."

"Everyone is always so busy during the Season."

"I find it tiresome, although there are compensations in all the diversions, I daresay. Not the routs and balls, but the theaters and concerts."

"Mama and I enjoy those, too," Araminta told her. "There is nothing so fine where we live, only small assembly rooms and occasional touring players."

"It is apparent we have a good deal in common, Miss Penrose. If you do have a spare hour one afternoon, I should be delighted if you'd call in at Grosvenor Square and take tea with me."

Araminta was naturally surprised at the invitation, having heard that Lady Betsey Barrington had scarcely a word to say for herself and no social life outside that allowed her by her husband. However, on the few occasions Araminta had been in her company, she had found her very pleasant, even though she was painfully shy.

"Of course," Lady Betsey added with characteristic uncertainty, "if you are too busy, I shall understand completely."

Araminta chuckled at the very notion. "Be assured, I shall not be too busy to call upon you, ma'am."

The woman's cheeks grew pink, and her eyes were bright with pleasure. "I shall look forward to it."

"No more than I."

Before she went into the shop, Araminta hesitated in the doorway, watching Lady Betsey hurry away to where her landau was waiting, and she was once again surprised, this time to see a gentleman awaiting her. Lady Betsey looked up at him and smiled, before he handed her into the carriage and followed her inside. However, although Araminta was surprised, she had learned since her arrival in town that strange liaisons often took place.

"I don't suppose that gentleman is her husband," Mary commented.

"That would be most unfashionable," her mistress replied, hiding a wry smile.

"Some coachman fellow tried to become familiar with me a little while ago, but I soon gave him a wigging...," the woman told her as Araminta went into the shop at last to choose her soaps.

Just as the carriage arrived back at the Penrose's rented house, the Duke of Avedon's curricle drew up behind it. Araminta flushed as he came to help her from the carriage. The memory of their last encounter was never far from her mind, how close they had been in the booth, the way he had kissed her hand, but just now she was anxious to learn how Dobbin was settling in to his new home. In fact, she had been so anxious, she had contemplated calling in at Avedon House to inquire.

His demeanor, she was glad to note, was warmer than on previous occasions. "I hoped to find you at home."

"You have news of Dobbin?" she asked anxiously.

"You seem more anxious about that mangy creature than a certain other matter," he teased.

"That is only because I am now resigned to the wait."

He looked somewhat surprised, but went on quickly, "Dobbin has settled in very well and is feeding regularly. In fact, he has an enormous appetite."

Araminta smiled with pleasure, and the duke continued, "He appears intent upon making up for all his deprivations and might yet live to a ripe old age."

"You have no notion what a great relief that is to me!"

"You might like to call in and see him whenever you wish. I should have made mention of that the other day, only I was a trifle taken aback by events."

She smiled happily. "I'm persuaded Dobbin is as grateful to you as I am, Your Grace."

"He has exhibited his gratitude by taking a fancy to one of my thoroughbred mares."

Araminta's hand flew to her lips. "Oh, my goodness!"

"As soon as he is strong enough, he'll be sent on to Summerhills, unless you want him to be sent to Middlehampton. He's your horse, so the decision rests entirely with you."

"I believe the good fresh air at Summerhills and the expert care of your grooms will be just what he needs."

"So be it. I can always send him to you when you are settled with an establishment of your own."

For a few moments, there was an awkward silence between then, and then Araminta said, "This must be the most dreadful nuisance to you, Your Grace."

He was already moving away from her. "Why should you think so? I'm considering turning Summerhills into a rest home for out-of-curl cattle. I daresay I can rely upon you to supply me."

She started to laugh as he climbed back onto the box. He raised his hat to her as he drove away, and then her smile became more wistful before she went into the house to present her mother with the gift she had bought her.

TWELVE

The Duke of Avedon's carriage drew away from the curb and His Grace sat back in the squabs to observe his guest. Aware of his scrutiny, but in no way embarrassed by it, Lady Westcot pulled her cloak around her and gazed at him as she said silkily, "I had almost given up hope that you would want to see me without a hundred others around us."

"I hope I would always want to see you."

The countess looked coy. "You have not once striven to seek some measure of intimacy since your return to town."

"There was much that concerned me when I first arrived. The house had been somewhat neglected for the past few years and needed all my attention."

"Valeria has told me that you have restored it to its former magnificence."

As he gazed across the carriage at her, his eyes were dark and brooding. "She is mistaken. It is much better than it was before."

Lady Westcot laughed. "That is so typical of you, Avedon! I cannot wait to see it for myself."

"Is not patience a virtue, ma'am?"

Again she laughed. "It is not one for which I am known."

His eyes twinkled. "Yes, I recall."

All at once she was serious again. "You, however, have extraordinary patience, I feel."

"It's true. I will wait an unconscionable time to get what I want."

"I cannot stress how much I admire that in you, but I cannot conceive of anything you might have wanted that was not immediately available to you."

She looked at him hopefully as he replied. "To achieve a flourishing of my estates was a long and difficult process after so many years of neglect. It involved an extraordinary amount of work."

She looked a little disappointed in his answer. "You achieved it in the end. As you say, you always get what you want eventually," she said, casting him a meaningful look.

He laughed. "I wish I could be as sure as you, my dear Lady Westcot."

"You know you can have everything your heart desires."

"How reassuring," he answered, and there was a bitter note to his voice.

Lady Westcot looked a little disgruntled as she asked, injecting some measure of wheedling into her manner, "Tell me, my dear Oliver, did you ever think of me while you were ruralizing?"

"Occasionally," he confessed.

"Only occasionally? How ungallant of you to say so, but did you, perchance . . . miss me a little?"

He laughed a little uneasily. "If I say my life was for the most part too full of more weighty matters, you will have to forgive me."

"Now that it is certain you are not plagued by

such obligations, mayhap you will be able to devote more time to pleasurable pursuits."

"I certainly hope so."

She smiled, casting him an inviting look. "You can rely upon me to assist you in any or all diversions you wish to pursue."

"My dear, is that fair to all the others who seek your company?" he asked, looking amused.

"Why do you care?" she asked pettishly. "You never used to care a fig about anyone."

"Yes," he answered heavily, "and it was a great fault in me, I confess. Let us not waste time upon what used to be, but enjoy what is now."

The sulk disappeared and she smiled again. No gentleman, he thought, could not be moved by her beauty.

"We must make up for all those empty years."

The duke looked surprised. "Empty, my lady? Your years with Charlie Westcot?"

Her ladyship was not abashed. "Charlie and I were happy enough, but you must be aware he was not my first choice of husband."

The duke was spared the necessity of replying as the carriage came to a halt outside the Hanover Square Rooms. The countess glanced out unenthusiastically, saying, "What an odd choice of venue, Oliver. I'd have thought you might prefer to attend the Langley-Smythe hurricane."

"That will be nothing out of the ordinary," the duke told her. "This, I fancy, is going to be quite a different diversion."

"I have a liking for Italian opera, providing it is interspersed with sufficient harlequinades and ballets to amuse," Lady Westcot admitted, "but I cannot abide too much of a maudlin nature. One is so easily bored."

"I haven't been bored in years." She cast him a curious look, and he smiled. "I'm persuaded you will find the evening's entertainment a little different."

"A concert of ancient music does not sound in the least diverting."

"The tickets are much sought after, and I consider myself fortunate having procured a pair."

He climbed down and then helped his beautiful companion out of the carriage. It was with great reluctance, she allowed him to relinquish her hand.

"I have it in mind," she confided as they went inside, "you have chosen this place because it is unlikely anyone will intrude upon us."

Araminta and her mother were already seated in the auditorium when the duke and Lady Westcot arrived to take their places.

Mrs. Penrose glanced at her daughter worriedly and said, "Minty, my dear, I cannot help but feel you have been out of countenance ever since your drive with His Grace the other day. You must tell me if he said anything untoward to you."

A strange look came upon Araminta's face at the mention of the duke's name. "On the contrary, Mama, he was at his most charming and obliging."

"That, I fancy, would not weigh with you in the prevailing circumstances."

"The more I come to know him, the stranger it seems that he withholds his consent. On the whole, he seems not particularly disagreeable. At times he is most agreeable. . . ."

"That is precisely my opinion of him, and I have always held the opinion that he could at any time change his mind and give his permission for Hal to marry. In fact, it is always possible he has written to Hal, giving him permission."

"Do you really think so?" Araminta was wide-eyed and agitated by the notion.

"I have not been able to see His Grace as unreasonable, Minty. After all, if he had been as stiff-rumped and starched as we envisaged at the outset, he would have cut us completely, instead of soliciting your company on several occasions and behaving in a most charming manner toward me. Your father, I fancy, would call him a great gun."

"I suspect he solicited our company in order to find us wanting."

Mrs. Penrose laughed disparagingly. "Perhaps the fault lies with Hal himself rather than with his guardian," she suggested a moment later.

Araminta looked aghast. "Mama! How can you say such a thing about Hal of all people?"

"You think him perfection, but I am persuaded he is no more that than any other gentleman."

"If the duke is about to relent and give his permission, I cannot help but wish he had told me of his decision first."

Mrs. Penrose smiled knowingly. "That is not the way of gentlemen, and not in the least necessary."

At that moment, Mrs. Penrose caught sight of the duke and Lady Westcot taking their seats. "Araminta," she whispered, nodding in their direction.

The young lady frowned. "How strange to see them here of all places. I would not have thought Handel and Haydn her kind of music. Lady Westcot cannot dance to any of it."

Mrs. Penrose chuckled. "How droll you are,

Minty. You really should not say such things, but she is a chucklehead, isn't she?"

"Gentlemen don't care how cork-brained a female may be, as long as she is fair of face."

Bella Penrose stared hard at her daughter in astonishment to hear such uncharacteristic bitterness issue from her lips. As Araminta averted her gaze from the newcomers and reverted to staring at her program card, her mother drew in a sharp breath.

"Minty, you haven't allowed yourself to become enamored of his charm, have you, dear?"

"I wouldn't be such a gudgeon," the girl replied, her voice husky.

"Oh, you have, haven't you? You poor child. What a case of pickles this has turned out to be."

"Was it not you who told me few females are able to resist his charm?"

"But not you, Minty. I'd have wagered a good deal that you would remain resistant especially in the circumstances."

Tears sparkled on the ends of Araminta's lashes, and she kept her head bowed. "What a peagoose I am. I was so well forewarned about his charm and manner of address. *I* had so much reason to take him in dislike, and yet as if I was some totty-headed female, I have succumbed utterly."

Mrs. Penrose sounded distraught as she whispered, "Minty, what are you to do? I cannot bear it if you are so unhappy."

"I would like to return to Middlehampton as soon as we can, Mama. I see no other solution."

"We cannot! Oh Minty, you cannot possibly return before the end of the Season. It would look so odd."

"I care nothing for that. It was futile coming here, and I recall telling you so at the outset, even though we have contrived to enjoy ourselves well enough."

"What shall I tell Lady Dunwoody? She has endeavored to ensure we receive so many invitations. Oh, that dreadful man! How could I have thought to like him? He seems to cut a devilish swath wherever he goes, and gives not a jot what heartache he leaves behind him."

Araminta put her hand out to still her mother's flow of invective. "Hush, Mama. In this instance, he is blameless. He cannot be held responsible for my foolishness."

Before Mrs. Penrose could comment further, the orchestra, which had assembled on the dais in front of the statue of Apollo, began to play. As the musicians struck up the national anthem, everyone arose, although there was some murmur of dissent among some members of the audience who found the Regent unpopular.

The duke was clearly visible during the anthem, a head taller than most others in the room. Araminta glanced at his proud profile, and her heart constricted painfully.

When everyone was once again seated, the first part of the concert began. Normally, Araminta would have enjoyed it, but on this occasion she was too much aware of the duke sitting in the audience accompanied by a woman popularly known as the most beautiful in London.

She knew she was not the first female to lose her heart to him, but Araminta felt she must be the most foolish, being forewarned as well as prejudiced against him. She was acting just like the cork-brained females she held in so much disdain, but she was determined he would never know he had stolen her heart. The tiresome Penrose pride would come to her assistance and save her from his scorn. That was her only consolation.

By the time Handel's oratorio had ended to the enthusiastic applause of the rest of the audience, Lady Westcot was tapping her foot with boredom. Her lovely face was set into a vexed frown.

She fluttered her fan in front of her face, saying, "I did not find that in the least diverting."

"How regrettable," the duke sympathized. "I thought it was quite splendid." When she cast him a surprised look, he added, placatingly, "I believe you'll find the second half more to your taste. It is, I believe," he consulted the program card with due consideration, "Haydn's Surprise Symphony!"

Lady Westcot's face relaxed from its petulant frown into a mischievous grin. "Let us then surprise everyone by leaving before it begins." Suddenly her smile froze as she glanced past him across the room where members of the audience were streaming out into the lobby.

"What are *they* doing here?"

The duke followed the direction of her gaze to where Araminta and her mother were in conversation. "Why, it's Mrs. Penrose and her daughter," he said, affecting surprise.

"Those dreadful, shabby-genteel females, so dull and boring, and with few redeeming features."

"Miss Penrose is an exceedingly good gamester," the duke told her, looking amused. "That surely is one redeeming feature."

"So, she is talented in one small area that is of no account."

"Far more than that—she is also a competent

whip." As Lady Westcot began to look even more vexed, he added, "As to why they are here, I daresay they have come for much the same reason as everyone else—to enjoy the concert. Shall we go out into the lobby for a while and see who we might encounter?"

She got to her feet, saying, "Such expertise is not becoming in a debutante, and I heartily pity her mother being obliged to launch such a drab little creature."

The duke cast her a mocking look. "It would be a dull world, my dear, if every female was as fetching as you. And, I beg of you, do not waste your pity on Mrs. Penrose, for she is aware that her daughter has already won the heart of a fine fellow who knows a jewel when he finds one."

Lady Westcot's eyes narrowed as she hesitated in the entrance to the hall. "Who is this fine fellow you're talking about, Oliver?"

The duke cast her a maddening smile. "I regret I cannot at present say."

He would have moved out into the lobby had she not put a hand on his arm to stay him. "You are being very provoking."

"I do not mean to be. Shall I procure a glass of lemonade for you?"

She threw back her head and laughed. "Lemonade? Ancient music? I declare you might well be quite a different gentleman to the one who left society a few years ago. I recall, as if it were yesterday, the times Charlie was obliged to escort you home because you were too foxed to find your own way." Her more customary alluring smile returned as she glanced past him. "Why, that is Archie Kilgannon over there. Who would have thought to see him here?"

Lady Betsey Barrington caught sight of her brother-in-law entering the lobby, and she pushed her way through the crowds to find him. However, when she reached the place she thought him to be, she found only Lady Westcot in conversation with the dandified Archie Kilgannon.

Lady Westcot smiled at her mockingly. "Why, Lady Betsey, imagine meeting you here."

"I thought I saw my brother-in-law," she stammered, blushing furiously.

"Oh, you did, my dear, but he is elsewhere now, and I am being diverted for the first time this evening by Mr. Kilgannon. Avedon is proving to be a dead bore. Is Lord John with you tonight?"

Lady Betsey looked discomforted. "My husband does not enjoy music."

The countess laughed. "He is a gentleman so full of good sense, my dear, at least in that respect." Lady Betsey's cheeks grew red as her ladyship added, "He and I always did have a good deal in common."

Lady Betsey raised her head proudly. "Mayhap I am seeking His Grace in the wrong company. I note that Miss Penrose is present this evening, and it is possible I shall more likely find him with her."

Lady Betsey inclined her head and turned away with Lady Westcot's mocking laughter ringing in her ears. As she pushed her way back through the crowds, she came face-to-face with the duke at last. "Hello, Betsey," he greeted her affably. "I had no notion you were here tonight."

"I am similarly surprised to see you. This kind of music is hardly the kind you would normally wish to hear, and I fancy Lady Westcot is of a similar opinion."

The duke looked skeptical. "Surely you are not trying to intimate that Lady Westcot is not enjoying her evening."

"She will enjoy your company, just as she enjoys Johnny's company and now that of Mr. Kilgannon and half the gentlemen of the ton." The woman bit her lip and looked away in confusion. "I do beg your pardon, Oliver. I had no right to say that to you."

"You really must strive not to apologize for plain speaking, my dear."

"I really would like to see you wed, Oliver, but not if it means marrying that woman. I was wrong to hope for such an outcome."

"Don't get into a pucker on that score, Betsey,"

"That nice Miss Penrose is much more suited," she ventured and then once again became embarrassed at the cold look that came onto his face. She started visibly when a young gentleman came up to her.

"Lady Betsey, I was wondering where you had got to."

She continued to look confused and embarrassed as she said, "This is Mr. Farthington, a close friend. My brother-in-law, His Grace the Duke of Avedon."

One of the duke's eyebrows rose slightly as the young man greeted him effusively. "I'm delighted to make your acquaintance, sir," the duke told him truthfully, satisfied that his errant brother was receiving the kind of treatment he was more used to dishing out.

Moreover, he considered that his sister-in-law deserved the attention her husband was unwilling to give her, and he resolved to pay Sir Leo his winnings at the earliest possible moment.

"I hope we'll have another opportunity to converse later. In the meantime, I must return to Lady Westcot."

He was still reeling somewhat from seeing his sister-in-law with a gentleman who appeared to be her *cher ami*, and was puzzled when he could find no sight of Lady Westcot where he had left her. However, he did catch sight of Mrs. Penrose, looking lost and bewildered among the throng.

"Mrs. Penrose," he greeted her, as she appeared unwilling to pause and speak to him.

After dithering for a moment or two, finally she smiled awkwardly. "Your Grace."

"Do you enjoy the concert, ma'am?"

"Exceedingly well. At Middlehampton the opportunity to hear such excellent music does not often present itself. We have, as you may know, only the smallest assembly rooms. Araminta and I are enjoying every opportunity presented here in town while we may."

"You must resolve to visit more often in the future."

Mrs. Penrose laughed uncomfortably. "I don't believe Araminta . . ."

All at once the duke frowned. "Have you by any chance seen Lady Westcot? I left her waiting hereabouts."

"Why yes. I saw her only a minute ago." She paused and then, when he frowned again, she added, somewhat diffidently, "I believe she was leaving. She was near the entrance and wearing her cloak."

The duke looked even more perplexed. "Was she by any chance alone?"

Again Mrs. Penrose hesitated before she answered, "I believe I saw her leaving with a gentleman I know as Mr. Kilgannon."

"Evidently she has become unwell," he replied in what Mrs. Penrose regarded as a remarkably lighthearted manner. "Would you care for some lemonade, ma'am?"

The woman blushed, "Indeed. I am obliged to you, Your Grace. I was not in the least looking forward to the crush."

"Is Miss Penrose not with you?"

Once again she appeared to be discomforted. "Araminta has elected to remain in her seat. She feels a trifle out of curl this evening and did not wish to brave the crush."

"How unlike her that is. When we last met, she was in high gig. What can have happened to put her out of countenance?"

Mrs. Penrose swallowed a mouthful of lemonade before she replied, unable to meet his worried gaze, "When the affections of a girl as loyal and constant as my daughter are engaged and she is uncertain of the outcome, she is bound to find herself in the mopes from time to time."

The woman watched him anxiously for a reaction, and wondered if she had been too rash in speaking out on her daughter's behalf.

A muscle tightened in his cheek as he replied, "You must not concern yourself for Miss Penrose's feelings, ma'am. I vow to you, she will not face a future wearing the willow."

Mrs. Penrose's habitual expression of unease turned to one of amazement and delight. "Your

Grace! I am so relieved, although I did suspect that might be the case."

The duke smiled, too, then. "Neither you nor Miss Penrose have any further cause for concern."

"I cannot adequately express my delight, although, I confess now, I did wonder the wisdom of making mention of it to you."

"I had already made up my mind. However, I would be very much obliged if you would keep the knowledge between the two of us until I have endeavored to speak with another party."

Once again Mrs. Penrose flushed with pleasure. "Oh, indeed, and I must venture to tell you, Araminta will make the most excellent of wives, Your Grace."

Unsmiling now, he replied, "I do not doubt it. In the meantime, with your permission, I would like to have words with her."

"Most certainly, Your Grace." She glanced around anxiously. "I shall remain here and seek out an acquaintance I caught sight of a little while ago."

Araminta's head remained bowed as the duke approached her seat. She only became aware of his presence when he was towering over her, and she looked up at him fearfully.

"Miss Penrose, I have brought you a glass of lemonade."

As she accepted the glass, she looked away from him again. "You are very kind to concern yourself, but you must not absent yourself from Lady Westcot."

"She will not mind. I hope you do not."

"By no means."

"You will be glad to know that Dobbin is making excellent progress."

"I am more than obliged to you, Your Grace," she murmured.

After a momentary hesitation, he asked, "May I sit down?"

She smiled foolishly. "I do beg your pardon. Please do."

"Araminta," he said softly when he was seated and she turned to look at him, her eyes wide and luminous. "May I call you Araminta?" He smiled faintly, and she longed to reach out and touch him. The recollection of their closeness at the fair was never far from her mind. "After all, we shall one day soon, in a sense, be related."

"You are giving your consent," she breathed.

"Yes." A strange expression crossed her face, and he asked, "Is that not what you wished?"

"Of course. You need not doubt that I am delighted."

"Then it is most satisfying for all," he said, his gaze never leaving hers. Her eyes became moist with tears, and the duke felt himself assailed by unusual emotions. Then adopting a more brisk manner, he added, "I thought I would leave within the next day or so, and travel down to Middlehampton to speak to Hal."

Her eyes grew wider. "Oh no." One of his eyebrows rose questioningly, and she looked away. "You must not." Then in the face of his obvious puzzlement, she added in a strangled tone, "Would it not be best if you wrote to him instead?"

"The matter is too important for that. Because of my opposition to his marriage, there has been some ill feeling toward me, and I would wish to meet Hal and put matters to rights. I should have known his choice of bride was a good one."

"How can you be so sure?" she asked.

He smiled grimly. "I have never been more certain about anything."

Araminta toyed with the cord of her reticule, and when she spoke again, her voice was only a choked whisper. "May I ask what has served to change your mind?"

"I came to realize that my opposition was based on unfounded fears for Hal."

"I see."

"I also came to appreciate how fortunate he was to possess the love and undivided loyalty of a female who has evidently enriched his life."

She turned sharply to look at him again, but he just got to his feet and took her hand in his. He raised it to his lips before saying, in almost a whisper, "What a pity there is another, Araminta." Then he turned her hand over to kiss the palm in a long, sensuous gesture.

Araminta remained speechless as he hurried out of the concert hall. When her mother joined her a few minutes later, Araminta was fighting back her tears.

"Minty, dearest! What can His Grace have said to put you out of countenance? He intimated to me he was about to impart some information that would please you."

"He did, Mama, he most certainly did. He is withdrawing his opposition to the wedding."

Mrs. Penrose sank down in her seat. "So that is what he meant, and I thought ..." She turned to give her daughter an encouraging smile. "We should both be delighted, Minty."

Still choking back her tears, Araminta murmured, "I am, Mama, I truly am."

THIRTEEN

Once Araminta had engaged Lady Betsey in general conversation over their tea, she found her to be a good deal more forthcoming than her reputation allowed. They discussed all manner of things, including several people of their acquaintance, and Araminta found her hostess possessed a lively wit.

"If you forgive my impertinence, my lady," Araminta ventured, "but was it difficult for you to grow used to being a part of the ton after your marriage?"

"It still is!" was the laughing reply. "Lady Stanyon and Lady Dunwoody, my sisters-in-law always seem rather alarming to me."

"To me, too," Araminta agreed over the tea served in dainty Minton cups.

"They are rather high in the instep, but not at all ill-natured," Lady Betsey was quick to assure her, "which cannot be said of everyone we encounter in the beau monde. An outsider with a fortune is often the object of scorn."

"Much as those without a fortune, even with modest connections."

Lady Betsey laughed again. "We have a good deal in common."

"Lady Dunwoody is procuring vouchers for Almacks for me, but it is of no account to me, for I'd liefer not go."

"Do not say so, Miss Penrose, for your debut has attracted a good deal of interest."

"I hadn't noticed," Araminta replied, to receive an odd look from her hostess, who urged her to help herself to the plum cake being handed around by a splendidly liveried servant.

Araminta could not help but note that the Barringtons lived in very great style. Although it was well-known that their luxurious life-style owed everything to Lady Betsey's fortune, Araminta was certain it was her husband who effectively spent it.

"I am rather partial to plum cake," Lady Betsey confided with the air of a naughty schoolgirl.

"So am I," Araminta confessed, drawing a sigh, for it was a great effort to hide her despondency. "At Middlehampton, our cook bakes a particularly fine plum cake."

"I can tell from your tone, Miss Penrose, that you enjoy the country."

"I have known little else, except for this brief stay in town."

"I always enjoy our sojourns in the country, but my husband, I'm afraid, is happier in town with access, of course, to all the diversions and his clubs."

"It is possible to enjoy both, is it not?"

Lady Betsey looked all at once sad before she ventured, "You are well acquainted with my brother-in-law, the Duke of Avedon, are you not?"

Araminta started at the mention of his name, to which she had become most sensitive of late. It was easy to overlook the connection between Lady Betsey and the duke. "I would not say we are well acquainted, ma'am, but his ward Henry Turlington and I most certainly are."

"I see," her hostess replied and appeared somewhat taken aback. "I had thought . . . I had hoped. You see, Oliver Avedon is dear to me. He has always been exceedingly kind to me. . . ."

Araminta looked surprised as the woman went on with her eyes downcast, "I had hoped this visit, so long overdue, meant that he had in mind . . . matrimony."

At this suggestion, Araminta felt her cheeks growing red. "That might well be true, if the tattle-baskets are to be believed, but I'm afraid you have entirely mistaken his interest in me."

Before Lady Betsey could reply, the door flew open, and Lord John came striding in. There was a good deal about him that reminded Araminta of the duke, who despite all his obvious failings, was preferable to Lord John, who seemed not to possess any of his brother's redeeming features and was selective upon whom he bestowed the famous Barrington charm.

"Betsey, another posy has been delivered to you. I am told it is the third this week."

His wife swallowed her tea before replying, "Four actually, dearest. Is that not kind?"

Surprisingly he held the flowers in his hand, as if they were about to catch fire and burn him. All at once he caught sight of Araminta and drew back.

"Miss Penrose, I do beg your pardon. I had no idea . . ."

Araminta put down her cup and got to her feet. "It really is time for me to go. I do thank you, Lady Betsey, for a most enjoyable coze."

"It has been congenial to me, too, dear. You must call upon me again and soon."

Araminta sketched a curtsy. Lord John bowed curtly, his brow furrowed into a frown. The footman let her out, and however enjoyable her conversation with Lady Betsey had been, she was glad to be away now that Lord John had arrived in what appeared to be a towering rage.

"What was *she* doing here?" Lord John demanded as soon as the door had closed behind Araminta.

"She was taking tea with me, dearest."

"Apparently at your invitation."

"Naturally. She appears close to your brother, and I thought it incumbent upon me to show her a little hospitality in the event he makes an offer for her."

"That is out of the question. His interest in her is of a different nature."

"I am not so sure. Your sisters, I'm persuaded, will only patronize the chit, and I did want to make her feel at ease. Entering the Barrington family is a very daunting matter, as I know too well."

"You are a fool, Betsey."

"Yes, dear, you often tell me so. Did you say that posy was for me or have you bought it for someone else?"

"You know full well it's for you. Who is sending these things?" he asked, exhibiting not only irritation, but a good deal of bewilderment, too.

She plucked the card attached to the posy. "Mr. Farthington. How kind of him to trouble himself just for me."

Lord John's face grew darker. "Sholto Farthington? That man milliner?"

"He is a little too dandified for good taste, isn't he? But there are few gentlemen who aspire to your heights of sartorial elegance, Johnny, and he does escort me to various diversions, which leaves you free to engage in all your favorite pursuits without being obliged to concern yourself with me."

Lord John was becoming even more perplexed and with uncharacteristic humility said, "You need not remind me, Betsey, for I have become aware of neglecting you somewhat of late."

"You mustn't think so, dearest," she assured him while she admired the flowers, "I have been assembling a circle of my own acquaintances of late, and I confess to being quite content."

"Even so," he went on with some difficulty, adjusting what was a perfectly folded neck cloth in the mirror, "I intend to take you out in my new phaeton this afternoon. It occurred to me you have yet to travel in it."

Lady Betsey looked up at him. "What a nice thought, Johnny. I would so love to go in your new phaeton. I have heard so much about it, but I'm afraid I cannot. Mr. Farthington is calling for me in half an hour's time, and it would not be at all the thing to cry off. Another day, perhaps?"

She moved toward the door, thrusting the posy at the footman as she went. "Put these in a vase, if you please."

She paused in the doorway to cast her husband a smile, leaving him frowning at his own reflection in the mirror. Only when she was out of sight, did she draw a sigh and look uncertain again.

Early the following morning, Lord John Barrington drove around to his brother's house to find the splendid green curricle beneath the porte cochere. The duke greeted him warily in the hall. He was dressed for a journey and looked upon his younger brother with some irritation.

"I hadn't looked to see you this morning, John," he said with some asperity.

"I was off to a mill at Islington. The Battling Scot against Will Siner, two excellent pugilists. I thought you might like to come along."

"So I would, but I'm leaving town for a day or two."

Lord John considered his brother curiously for a moment or two before he glanced outside at the two splendid carriages and said, "We cut a swath just like we used to do. Apollo and Cupid. Do you recall?"

"That was before you became better known as Black Jack Barrington."

The younger man laughed. "I do believe I prefer that!"

"Cut line, Johnny. I'm off to Middlehampton, and am anxious to be on my way."

"Middlehampton?"

"Unfinished business with my ward."

"Ah! Would that be connected to Miss Penrose by any chance?"

The duke looked surprised. "It might. Who told you about her?"

"Miss Penrose did."

"After you had quizzed her closely no doubt."

"It was just my brotherly concern, Oliver. I thought you were fixing your interest, however unlikely that seemed to be."

"That wouldn't be in your interest, would it? Well, is that all you came here to ask?"

"Good grief, no! I just wanted to solicit some advice, that's all, but that's really of no account." He frowned then. "You're riding grub this morning, Oliver. Is something wrong?"

The duke was immediately regretful. "I beg your pardon for that, Johnny. You'd better come into the study." Once ensconced, the duke asked, "Would you like some refreshment?"

"No, I thank you, and I don't wish to delay you longer than necessary, but I'm concerned about Betsey."

The duke frowned. "*Betsey?* You're actually concerned about your wife, Johnny? This is a facet of your nature that has been hitherto hidden from me."

"Now, *you* cut line, Oliver," his brother warned, looking annoyed.

"Very well. What's amiss? She was in high gig when I saw her the other evening."

He seated himself facing his brother as Lord John said with great difficulty, "She's acting oddly."

The duke smiled at last. "In your eyes she always does, but it is a great improvement to note that you are concerned."

"Don't roast me, Oliver. She's taken a *cher ami*."

"Sholto Farthington?"

The man's eyes opened wide. "You *know*?"

"Not really, only I did see them together the other evening at the Hanover Square Rooms."

"You were there?" the younger man asked in astonishment, and then he began to shake his head. "Everyone must know. Betsey has a *cher ami*, and I shall be a laughing stock."

"I don't see why you should think so. It is not so out of the ordinary."

"For Betsey it is," his brother retorted with a mirthless laugh.

"You have your own diversions, and you've never concerned yourself for your wife before."

"She's always in high snuff these days. I've never seen her like that."

"It's amazing what a little attention can do for the female vanity," the duke answered wryly. "You must know that full well with all your female acquaintances."

"She's acting like a goosecap."

Restlessly the duke got to his feet. "Johnny, I really don't see why this is teasing you so, but given the choice, I am certain your wife prefers your company to that of Sholto Farthington, only you are so rarely available to her."

Lord John got to his feet, too. "Do you really think so, Oliver?"

"Yes, I do. Betsey has always harbored a great fondness for you."

Once again the young man shook his head woefully. "I suppose I am obliged to shoulder the blame. I haven't been a good husband, you know."

The duke smiled wryly. "Yes, I do know, but it isn't too late to make a new start if that is what you really want."

"Do you really think so?"

"Fidelity is becoming fashionable—or so I am told."

The duke flung an arm around his brother's shoulders and began to lead him toward the door. "If it teases you so much, resolve to spend so much time in Betsey's company that she will have no opportunity to be with Farthington. He will put up no fight, I assure you."

"You've always known how to behave with females, Oliver. I've always admired that in you."

The duke's laughter had a bitter tinge to it. "How
kind of you to say so!"

"It's true, even though there were those who were
making much of your attention to the Penrose chit,
I knew all the while she was not your style." He
glanced at him speculatively as they paused in the
doorway. "I can't say the same of Pammy Westcot,
though. Any man who wins her, gains a great prize,
providing, of course, he is willing to overlook the
matter of her flirtatious nature."

The duke moved toward his curricle, looking
mildly amused at his brother's probing. "With her
beauty and fortune, Johnny, a mild flirtatiousness
can always be overlooked."

"I'm not so certain I could be so magnanimous,"
the other man persisted, much to the duke's further
amusement. "It used to infuriate poor Charlie. It's
said they had an argument just before his accident,
over one of her ladyship's favorites, and that is why
he rode so recklessly. It wasn't characteristic of
him, you'll own."

He paused to cast his brother another speculative
look, but the duke just climbed up onto the box of
his curricle. "You really must stop joining the gab-
blegrinders for cat-lap, Johnny, and attend to the
needs of your wife. I shall see you in a day or two
when I return to town."

Lord John bit back a cry of annoyance as his
brother flicked his whip over the backs of his team,
and drove out of the carriage drive and into Piccadilly.

FOURTEEN

The journey to Middlehampton was an ideal opportunity for the duke to give his team of horses their head, something virtually impossible within the confines of town. He drove them hard in an effort to exorcise his own involved emotions, for once his amusement at his brother's predicament had worn off, he became preoccupied with his own situation.

He found it ironic that the girl his sister had described as having no consequence had so easily stolen his heart. Who would have believed it? No one of his acquaintance would credit it, so it was just as well the fact would never be known.

With his permission, if not his wholehearted blessing, Araminta Penrose would marry her adored Hal without further delay and, no doubt, raise a clutch of children, one of which was likely to become his godchild. The secret of his own feelings would stay locked within his heart forever. As he drove his team on even harder, the duke smiled grimly to himself. Some would regard it as justice after all the hearts he had, albeit unwittingly, broken in the past.

The recognition of his own feelings was the catalyst that made him decide to withdraw his opposition to the marriage. If he had remained in opposition to his ward's wishes, he knew it would only be because he coveted Araminta for himself.

When he entered the carriage drive of Mapplewood House, it was with a feeling of relief he saw the once familiar gray building in the distance. It had been a long time since his last visit, but he had enjoyed many happy times there, and it pleased him to reflect that before too long, the house would be filled with laughter again, just as it had been when Perry Turlington had been alive.

Caroline Turlington greeted her unexpected visitor with disbelief. "Oliver! I can't believe it's really you. What a surprise!"

"Caroline, my dear, you look not a day older than when we last met."

He kissed her on both cheeks, and she drew away to answer wryly, "That was a very long time ago." She frowned then. "I do trust that this unexpected visit does not mean that something is amiss."

"On the contrary. As long as I have not arrived at an inconvenient time, I would like to have words with Hal, and then leave for London first thing in the morning."

"You are, of course, welcome at Mapplewood at any time, Oliver, just as you were when Hal was a child and, indeed, when Perry was alive, but as for speaking to Hal ... well, frankly, he is not here."

That possibility hadn't occurred to him, and he looked vexed. "He has not gone to London, has he, Caroline?"

"Definitely not." In the face of such certainty,

he stared at her and she added, looking a little uncomfortable, "He declared often he could not bear to observe, what he called town sparks, paying court to Miss Penrose, and when he received the letter from you reiterating your opposition to their marriage, he was so out of curl, he decided to take himself off. You really have caused us considerable distress with your intransigence, Oliver."

"Us, Caroline?"

She flushed slightly. "You should not have dismissed his request out of hand. Hal may be young, but he is not foolish."

"I have come to understand that, Caroline." He paused before asking, "Are you fond of Miss Penrose?"

"Well, naturally I am. Hal has been acquainted with her and her family since childhood. She is a delightful child, and the family most respectable. He couldn't have made a better match." She frowned slightly. "You must have met her in town. She has been there for some time. Do you not agree?"

"Yes," he answered heavily, "and I have relented. That is what I wished to tell him."

"Oh, I am so glad!" Mrs. Turlington exclaimed, clapping her hands together.

"So, if you'll be obliging as to tell me where he is to be found just now, I'll go to see him and not trouble you any further."

Mrs. Turlington looked stricken. "That is the problem, Oliver. I don't know where he is! He merely told me he was going to visit friends and would write to me presently. I do expect to hear from him any day now."

"Hell and damnation!" the duke exclaimed under his breath, and then to Caroline Turlington, "What am I to do?"

"You are welcome to remain here until he returns. I'm persuaded it will be soon. He has been gone for almost two weeks."

A look of resignation crossed the duke's face. "I daresay I owe him that, Caroline."

"Your old room is ready for you, and dinner will be served in an hour. I shall have it put back until you are rested and refreshed." As he moved toward the stairs, she added softly, "I always knew your innate sense of fairness would prevail in the end."

The duke smiled ironically as he turned away and went up the stairs. When he came down again an hour later, dressed for dinner and refreshed after his journey, he was assailed by a maudlin feeling. One of the reasons he visited Mapplewood so rarely was not so much the pressure of his own affairs, but the memories of so many happy times here when Perry Turlington was alive.

A footman opened the door, and when the duke stepped into the drawing room, he was surprised to find Caroline sharing a sofa with a gentleman who immediately got to his feet. He was tall and elegant with thick gray hair and an amiable manner that immediately communicated itself to the duke.

Caroline Turlington looked all at once shy. "Oliver, permit me to present my neighbor and dear friend, Sir Mark Charrington."

The man bowed low. "I am delighted to make your acquaintance at last, Your Grace. Both Caroline and Hal have spoken of you often."

"Kindly, I hope," the duke murmured, glancing at his hostess, who had retained a good deal of her youthful beauty, and on this occasion looked positively girlish.

"Oh yes, you may be sure of it!" Sir Mark replied with a laugh.

"If I don't know you, Sir Mark, it is clearly evident that I have been away from Mapplewood too long."

"Have I not been saying so?" Caroline replied, looking flushed and pleased. "Shall we go in to dinner now?"

"I am famished," the duke admitted as they went into the dining room. "Post-inn food is never as good as it might be, and I recall the table at Mapplewood is always excellent."

Caroline Turlington sat at the end of the table with the two visitors on either side of her facing each other.

"Caro tells me you are sanctioning Hal's wedding at last," Sir Mark commented as they began their meal.

"I can see no good reason to withhold my permission any longer."

"Hal will be overjoyed, but you also have *my* eternal gratitude also, Your Grace."

The duke paused to glance at him. "Forgive me for asking, but how does it concern you, sir?"

Sir Mark glanced at Mrs. Turlington, who grew rather flushed, then he returned his attention to the duke. "I asked Caro to marry me a long time ago. She readily agreed, but only on the proviso I was prepared to wait until Hal was married."

"My felicitations to you both," the duke responded, looking somewhat surprised.

"It was always evident to me that Hal would marry the Penrose girl as soon as they were both old enough. Even as children they were inseparable, and I truly did not wish to leave Mapplewood until he was properly settled. Now I shall be able to devote myself to being Mark's wife."

"I had no notion, believe me," the duke assured her.

"Would it have swayed you if you had?" she asked.

"Probably not," he responded, prodding his meat in a disconsolate manner with his fork. "I could not in all conscience give my consent until I had assured myself that Miss Penrose was all Hal had said she was. I owed that to him, you, and not the least Perry."

"In your view, is she all that he said she was?" Mrs. Turlington asked.

"No" was the duke's unequivocal answer. "She was quite unlike his description of her in any respect."

"Good grief!" Sir Mark declared, glancing at his loved one. "I am beginning to wonder if Hal didn't make a mull of it when she solicited His Grace's permission. It wouldn't surprise me if he did, the gull-catcher."

Caroline Turlington laughed. "Hal has always been a mite willful, not to say stubborn, but it is of no consequence now."

The duke forced some brightness into his voice, "There are to be two weddings rather than the one I expected. That could not be better."

"Better still if we also had yours to look forward to, Oliver," Mrs. Turlington chided, "but I fear we have lost all hope of it."

"I am," he declared bleakly, "an incorrigible bachelor."

"I can heartily recommend marriage, Your Grace," Sir Mark told him. "After a lifetime of bachelordom, I am in a fidge to enter the parson's pound."

The duke cast a smile at his hostess. "I don't blame you in the least, Charrington. Caroline is a wonderful woman."

"I can't tell you how much I admired her stance over Hal, even though I've often despaired that we would ever get married. It's not as if Hal was ever a problem, not like some young sparks, but she insisted on remaining here at Mapplewood until he was safely buckled."

"When the time came, I was going to ask you to give me away, Oliver," Mrs. Turlington ventured. "Both Mark and I would be so pleased if you would."

It would also be another opportunity to witness Hal and Araminta's happiness. He sighed, then replied, "It will be my great pleasure, my dear."

"I can hardly wait for Hal to know of all this good news," his mother said delightedly as the dishes were removed in preparation for the puddings to be brought in. "I do hope wherever he is staying, he is not too despondent."

Neither of the gentlemen had any opportunity to reply before a flustered footman burst into the room. He in turn was given no opportunity to say anything before a rotund, red-faced gentleman came scuttling in on his heels.

As Sir Mark and the duke stared at him in astonishment, Mrs. Turlington got to her feet, clutching her napkin in her hands.

"Mr. Penrose, what on earth warrants this intrusion?"

At the mention of the name, the duke also got to his feet.

"Mrs. Turlington," the man said breathlessly, "I beg your pardon, but I have received the gravest shock and was obliged to come over to Mapplewood immediately!"

Mrs. Turlington clasped the back of the chair. "Oh, my goodness. What is it?"

"May I sit down? I feel quite indisposed. The shock . . ."

Before permission was granted, he pulled out a chair and sank into it. The duke went to fetch him a glass of brandy, which the fellow accepted gratefully.

"What can have put you in such a taking, sir?" Sir Mark asked.

"Oh, do not say something has happened to Hal!" Mrs. Turlington cried.

"Not until I get hold of him," Mr. Penrose vowed, and the observers exchanged curious glances. Then Mr. Penrose waved a piece of paper he had clutched in his hand. "Married!" he wailed. "My little girl abducted and taken to Gretna! I'll have his hide for this, just see if I don't!"

Mrs. Turlington frowned at the incomprehensible farrago, and then she snatched up the offending missive. As she read it, a smile came to her face. "It's true! Oh, do listen to this, both of you! Hal is in Gretna. Well, at least he was when this was written. Now they are married, they are on their way to London for their honeymoon!"

Sir Mark's face also broke into a smile. "Who would have thought it?"

"How could that young cub do such a thing!" Mr. Penrose wailed.

"It was as much your fault as anyone's," Mrs. Turlington accused. "You insisted that she make her debut, even though it was only a matter of time before they could be married. And may I also say, if anyone was abducted, it is more likely to have been my son!"

Throughout the exchange, the duke continued to look perplexed. At last he could contain himself no longer and demanded to know, "What is going on?"

"It appears that Hal and Miss Penrose have eloped to Gretna!" Sir Mark explained.

"That's impossible!" the duke declared. "I was with Araminta only the other evening. There has been no time for her to go to Gretna and get married."

Mrs. Turlington and her future husband looked startled. Mr. Penrose shot the duke an angry look. "And who, sir, are you?"

Almost absently Mrs. Turlington said, "This is His Grace, the Duke of Avedon."

This pronouncement caused Mr. Penrose to splutter into his brandy glass. "It was you who . . ."

Mrs. Turlington waved one hand in the air. "Oh, don't trouble your head about that now. Let us join together to celebrate the marriage of my son to Fanny. What is done is done, and we must all be glad of the outcome."

"Why do you call her Fanny?" the duke insisted, feeling he could well be in one of the cells at Bedlam sharing it with a group of lunatics. "And I am telling you categorically I was with her less than two days ago."

"Is it true, after all, he is a gibbering lunatic, Mrs. Turlington?" Mr. Penrose asked. "Why is he going on about Araminta?"

"Why are *you* talking about Fanny?" the duke responded, his patience rapidly running out now.

"Because Fanny is Hal's . . . wife now, I daresay," his hostess pointed out in some bewilderment.

"Do not speak to me of that treacherous Minty, or my sister-in-law, Bella, to whom I entrusted my precious child!"

At last the duke was beginning to comprehend, but he dared not yet trust what was starting to emerge.

"Do you mean to tell me there are two Miss Penroses in London?" he asked.

"There were supposed to be," Mr. Penrose replied, continuing to look aggrieved. "As my child is motherless and Araminta of a similar age, I entrusted her to my sister-in-law to bring out, and provided the wherewithal to do so! I have been betrayed!"

"Araminta," the duke breathed.

"You did not think Araminta and Hal . . . ?" Mrs. Turlington began. "Of course, Minty is the most delightful girl, and Hal and she are great friends, but there has never been anyone except Fanny for my son."

"Fanny, the beauty and the heiress," the duke chuckled.

"Fanny has sent me regular letters since she left for London," Mr. Penrose complained, "and I daresay that minx Araminta is responsible for *that*." He shot an accusing look at the duke. "You opposed the match. What are you going to do about it now?"

His Grace glanced at his hostess and then to the two other men. "With Mrs. Turlington's permission, I suggest we break open a bottle of champagne, and I will propose a toast to weddings! Lots of them!"

FIFTEEN

Because of the lateness of the hour, they retired, and the amount of champagne that was consumed in celebrating the nuptials of Miss Fanny Penrose and Henry Turlington, it was much later than planned that the duke left Mapplewood House the following morning.

His head ached, and he was unable to eat any breakfast, save for a cup of coffee. In the years since he had left his roistering youth behind, the duke had to acknowledge, sadly, that he was no longer able to spend a night drinking and be bright the following morning.

Caroline Turlington escorted him out to the carriage, fussing like a mother hen. "Now you did promise to return for my wedding, Oliver. You will endeavor to do so, won't you?"

"You already have my word on it, Caro."

She smiled happily before she became anxious again. "I do trust you won't ring too much of a peal over Hal's head, should you encounter him in London."

"You have my word on that, too, my dear."

She watched him drive away, waving her handkerchief until he was out of sight. Instead of driving straight for the Great North Road and London, he took a short diversion to Plumstead Park, the home, until her marriage, of Miss Fanny Penrose. He found Mr. Penrose in a pensive mood.

"I just called in to assure you," the duke told him, "that I shall keep a keen eye on the young couple for the time being."

"I'm much obliged to you, Avedon," the man responded. "I shall miss the chit, I confess. She's my only child. Her mother passed away when Fanny was very small. This is a great blow to me, even though I knew it must happen one day. I had hoped to keep her with me a little longer. I thought sending her to London for the Season would delay her marriage to that young cub."

As he shook his head mournfully, the duke slapped him heartily on the back. "Do cheer up, Penrose. She'll be back, and no doubt bring with her a clutch of grandchildren to cheer your old age."

When the duke left Plumstead Park, Mr. Penrose was somewhat cheerier than before, anticipating a pleasant future surrounded by his grandchildren. His Grace's second place of call was less easy to find, but after resorting to stopping at an inn to ask directions, he found the home belonging to the other Mr. Penrose just outside the small town of Middlehampton.

It was altogether smaller than Fanny Penrose's house, but as it was Araminta's home, the duke liked it immediately. He climbed down from the curricle in a leisurely fashion; it hurt his head less that way. But he was also able to survey the house Araminta was so anxious to return to with great care.

As far as he could see, it bore no historical or

architectural qualities, but was no doubt comfortable in a shabby way. As he slowly approached the porticoed door, a sound of barking preceded a large dog, which came bounding around the corner and hurled himself at the duke's immaculate form.

After allowing himself to be assaulted for a brief moment, he recovered sufficiently to say, "Down! Down I say!" in his most authoritative manner.

The animal obeyed, sitting on his hind legs and gazing at the duke with adoration. "What a useless animal you are."

The dog responded by thumping his tail on the ground. The duke brushed off his pantaloons before continuing on his way to the front door, only to find the dog in close attendance. He seized the knocker and wielded it with rather more ferocity than he would normally employ, keeping his eye on the dog all the while should he be forced to fend off another demonstration of affection from that quarter.

The maidservant who took his card was noticeably overawed by the important appearance of the visitor, and she scuttled away after he had said, "Be pleased to inform Mr. Penrose that the Duke of Avedon wishes to see him. And when you return, will you make certain this creature does not follow me in?"

Ensconced in his study, Mr. Gerald Penrose frowned at the card without really seeing it. "Have you seen my book of accounts anywhere, Celia?"

"No, sir. I wouldn't know it anyhow, for I can't read."

"Oh, how I wish Mrs. Penrose were here! Nothing has been right since she left for London. She would insist upon Araminta coming out, but that was only because Fanny was making her debut and my brother Hubert offered to pay their shot. It is a complete waste of time, I'm sure, for Minty has too much good sense to settle for some man milliner, for that is all she will meet in those circles. Now, what is this about a visitor, Celia?"

"He says he's the Duke of Avedon."

"The Duke of Avedon?" Mr. Penrose repeated, tapping the card thoughtfully. "I've never heard of the fellow. Do you know what he wants?"

"A few words with you, he said, sir," the maidservant assured him. "He's proper Quality and no mistake. Top o' the trees, I should say. I never was so betwattled as when I saw him standing there on the doorstep. He's a giant, too. Couldn't see the top of his head, even though I did crane my neck."

The alarming description notwithstanding, Mr. Penrose said vaguely, "You'd better show him in here, and I trust he isn't the bailiff in a jovial mood."

When the duke was shown into the study, he seemed to fill the tiny room. "Mr. Penrose?"

The other man began what the duke suspected was a habitual dither. "Your Grace, I'm afraid . . ."

"I shan't take up much of your time, sir, and with your permission, I shall get to the point."

"Please do. Time is very precious to all of us."

"I've called today regarding your daughter . . ."

Mr. Penrose looked startled. The duke thought he must always appear startled. "Do you know my daughter?"

The duke smiled at last. "I do have that pleasure, sir, and I'm asking your permission to address her."

189

Mr. Penrose frowned. "Araminta? Are you certain it isn't Fanny you're talking about?"

"Absolutely not, sir. Araminta it is."

The fellow looked a little lost for words, but then he said, "I think you should know, we are dreadfully poor. My brother, Hubert, has footed most of the expenses for Araminta's Season because Fanny is being launched with her."

"Mr. Penrose, your daughter's financial circumstances are of no account whatsoever. Allow me to tell you a little of my circumstances instead. I have an estate in Sussex of some ten thousand acres, together with sundry other properties that currently reap an income. . . ."

"Really, really," the older man muttered. "There is no need for such candor, I assure you. Whatever your circumstances, I fancy they must be greater than mine." He chuckled. "This is quite a surprise to me, Your Grace."

"To me too, sir," the duke replied dryly. "I have never been in love before."

Gerald Penrose stroked his chin. "In love with Minty, eh? Well, well, well. How extraordinary."

"Are you pleased, sir?"

"Pleased? Oh yes, yes indeed. I'm very pleased. She has an excellent disposition and deserves everything of the best."

"If she condescends to marry me, she will have everything her heart desires. At least, as much as I am able to provide for her."

"She has very modest needs," her father pointed out. He then murmured, "This is splendid, splendid."

"Do I take it I have your permission, sir?"

Mr. Penrose nodded his head. "I don't know if

Minty has given her affections elsewhere. She hasn't troubled to tell me, but if she is receptive to your suit, I see no reason why I shouldn't give my blessing." Then he added, "Will you take some refreshment with me, Your Grace? The house isn't running very smoothly without Mrs. Penrose, but I daresay something can be arranged."

"Don't trouble, sir. I want to be on my way to London with no further delay."

"Very wise," the man concurred, ushering to the door.

As the curricle rattled down the drive, Mr. Penrose scurried back to his study, muttering, "How extraordinary. He wants to marry Minty."

Calling upon the two Penrose brothers caused the duke to arrive back in London much later than he had hoped. Furthermore, the journey turned out to be a filthy one, so he was obliged to go home first and bathe, and effect a complete change of clothing. So impatient was he to confront Araminta, he had originally intended to drive directly to her house.

However, when he did at last drive into Berkeley Street, he felt unaccountably nervous. Araminta may not, after all, be in love with Hal or he with her, but that did not mean she would be willing to consider him as a suitor. And, if his memory served him right, he recalled there had been some mention of a suitor in Middlehampton, someone Araminta missed very much during her stay in London.

When he entered the house, he had only just had time to take off his hat when Hal Turlington himself came out of the drawing room, closing the door carefully behind him.

"Hal!" the duke exclaimed, and the young man started guiltily.

There had been a faint smile on his face, but that immediately disappeared, and his cheeks flushed to a dull red. "Oliver, I did intend to call upon you in Piccadilly as soon as we were rested."

"You would have found me out, and you might as well know, I was at Mapplewood when Mr. Penrose arrived with your letter, so I know just where you've been for the past two weeks."

"You have evidently come to ring a peal over me, so you might as well get it over with, for I regret nothing!"

"Hal," the duke said in a gentle tone, "I only want to wish you happy."

"You do?" the young man asked incredulously.

"I confess, I have been acting like a lobcock over this. I only regret you were obliged to go to such lengths, truly I do."

The young man smiled broadly. "Thank you, Oliver. I always knew you were a nail. Fanny and I will want you as godfather to our first child."

The duke laughed and held up his hand. "If you have any regard for me, pray don't give me responsibility for any more Turlington youngsters."

Hal laughed, too. "Allow me then to buy dinner for you tonight at Greniers. I'm told they serve the best dinner in town."

"That would be most agreeable, only an April gentleman should not be out and about as yet."

"I have no intention of keeping late hours, you understand, but I do know Fanny and her cousin are in something of a fidge to discuss important matters such as gowns, pelisses, and the like."

A noise on the stairs caused them both to turn

around to see the two young ladies hesitating to come down. The duke raised his quizzing glass to study Hal's bride the better. Of course, Fanny Turlington was exactly as she ought to be. There was a faint resemblance to Araminta, but Fanny's beauty was extraordinary. The eyes beneath the brim of her bonnet were of the deepest blue, fringed by long, dark lashes. Her nose was straight and small, and her mouth, apparently permanently set into a rosebud shape, was all framed by a heart-shaped face. In the duke's opinion, if she'd made her debut, she would have caused a sensation in the ton. No wonder Hal was anxious to keep her away from those who might seek to turn her head.

She paused on the stairs, looking at her husband with some uncertainty, while the duke considered the picture of perfection she presented. Then when Hal said, "Fanny, dearest, allow me to introduce my guardian, His Grace, the Duke of Avedon."

Fanny Turlington came down the rest of the stairs, followed by an anxious-looking Araminta. When she sketched a curtsy, she said, "You must be very angry with us, Your Grace."

As she straightened up, she looked at him from beneath her long, dark lashes, and he could have laughed, for it was evident Fanny Turlington had spent a brief lifetime wheedling gentlemen, starting with her father and Hal.

"On the contrary, my dear," the duke assured her, "I could not be more delighted."

He kissed the girl on both cheeks and was aware that Araminta let out a long breath "Moreover, to indicate my approval, I have a house in Henrietta

Street that I intend to present to you as a wedding gift."

Mrs. Turlington clapped her hands together in delight as her husband said, "What a great gun you are, to be sure. In fact, we shall not only appoint you godfather to our firstborn, but call our first son for you!"

"Oh no, please . . ." the duke begged, laughing as he did so.

"I insist upon it, too," the bride declared. "It will be our privilege. Our first daughter, however, will be named for my dear cousin, Araminta. Without her assistance, we should not have contrived so well."

While Fanny beamed at her, Araminta averted her eyes. "So I am given to understand," the duke answered, giving his attention to her at last.

"Much as we would wish to remain here and talk with you further," Hal told him, "I promised Fanny we would go on a tour of the sights. She has never been to London before, and is in a fidge to acquaint herself with all she has been told about by her cousin."

"Minty really has whetted our appetites," the new bride confessed.

"Don't let me detain you a moment longer. There is, indeed, so much for you to see."

As the newlyweds went toward the door, Fanny paused to say shyly, "Mayhap you will condescend to stay with us at Mapplewood House when we return—if it will not bore you."

He glanced at Araminta, who remained with her eyes downcast, and then replied, "I fancy it won't do that."

The moment they had gone, he said to Araminta, "You must be delighted at the outcome."

"Indeed, I am," she breathed and then, stealing a glance at him, she added, "They were born to be together, I promise you."

"Yes, I believe that is true of some people. Miss Penrose—Araminta—may I speak with you in private?"

She drew herself up as straight as possible. Her expression was one of defiance, her manner resolute. "There is no need for that, Your Grace. I am fully aware you wish to remonstrate with me, but I am bound to tell you, I regret nothing!"

A faint smile curled his lips. He glanced at the maidservant, eagerly listening to every word, and he reiterated firmly, "In private, Miss Penrose."

After hesitating some few further moments, she turned on her heel and led the way into the tiny drawing room. "You must forgive Mama's absence," she said stiffly, "but she is somewhat overset by recent events and is resting in her room."

"That gives me a much needed opportunity to speak with you alone."

When she turned to face him, she appeared to be composed with her hands clasped firmly in front of her.

"Why don't we sit down?" he suggested.

"Be pleased to do so, Your Grace."

When she realized he was waiting for her to sit down first, she perched uneasily on the edge of the sofa, and after hesitating initially, he sat down at the other end.

"You are perfectly entitled to scold me for my part in deceiving you," she said, "and I would just wish you to do it now and get it over."

"I have no intention of scolding you," he retorted, and she looked up at him then in some surprise before he went on. "However, I would be interested to know the answers to one or two questions that still puzzle me."

Looking more than a little suspicious, Araminta answered, "I see no reason why you should not know everything now."

"I appreciate why you colluded with your cousin and my ward in this matter, but whatever her sympathies, I would not have expected a lady of Mrs. Penrose's sensibilities to aid and abet two runaway lovers."

"Mama did not!" Araminta declared. "She knew nothing of the matter until they arrived here yesterday. Mama thought Fanny was suffering a mystery illness that kept her at Middlehampton."

"I am given to understand, you kept sending her father Fanny's letters from London."

Araminta was pleating the fabric of her striped poplin gown between her fingers, and her lips quirked into a smile. "Yes."

"If I recall correctly, on one occasion you did it in front of me, did you not?"

Again the faint smile. "Yes."

"How was the ruse contrived?"

"When it was time for us to leave for London, Fanny affected an indisposition and was unable to accompany us. Once we were safely settled, Fanny recovered her health and was dispatched to follow, only the carriage picked up Hal as it passed through Middlehampton. After that, they traveled northward on the Great North Road rather than south. It was quite simple. All I had to do was keep sending Fanny's prepared letters to Uncle Hubert."

196

"Am I also to understand that this entire farrago was your idea, Araminta?"

She looked up at him then. "Yes, it was."

"My compliments on the effectiveness, ma'am," he said ironically. "I can now easily understand why you didn't feel the need to discuss the matter with me or beg me to allow them to marry. You knew all the while they were in Gretna Green."

"I thought it served you right to be bubbled." She looked up at him then, her strange little face animated. "I really am so sorry."

"So you ought to be. I really didn't deserve that Turkish treatment."

"I know," she admitted.

"Well, it is of no matter now. They are married and will live happily for the rest of their lives, and Mrs. Turlington and Sir Mark will soon be legshackled." There was a speculative pause before he added, "They do say these things come in threes."

She cast him a puzzled look, and he went on, "Before I came back to town, I called upon your father . . ."

"Papa!" she gasped.

"Araminta, he gave me leave to address you . . ."

Her hands flew to her reddening cheeks. "Me? I don't understand."

"It's quite simply because I love you. Why else would I endure an evening at the Hanover Square Rooms in the company of Lady Westcot?"

She continued to look disbelieving. "You must be aware that I have no portion."

"If it ever became necessary to raise the wind, all I need do is sit you at a gaming table. You will earn your own portion in a trice."

She laughed. "Now you are roasting me."

"You deserve it after your humgumption toward me. Of course, if there is someone else . . ."

"You know there is no one. How could there be? You have seen the little interest my debut has generated among likely suitors."

"When we drove in Hyde Park, you did say there was someone in Middlehampton."

"There are many gentlemen I regard as true friends, but no one of a romantic nature. . . ."

"I thought it was Hal."

"Hal?" She cast him a scornful look. "How could you think me such a peagoose? He has always adored my cousin. You couldn't possibly think I harbored a fondness for him."

He drew a sigh. "Until I went to Middlehampton, I thought you *were* Hal's bride-to-be."

"I am not in the least like Fanny. She is, as you have seen, a beauty, and she also possesses a fortune."

"I was not acquainted with Fanny, nor did I know that two of you were going to make your debuts this Season. When Miss Penrose was pointed out to me, I naturally assumed you were Hal's bride-to-be."

She clapped her hands to her lips to suppress a laugh. "How delicious! I had no notion you thought that, but it's now evident why you were so persistent in your attentions."

"At first, perhaps, but later it was for the pleasure of your company alone."

She smiled shyly then before she suddenly cried out, "I remember speaking of someone I loved who I left behind. It was, of course, Max. I missed him so much when we first arrived in London. In Middlehampton we are inseparable. I do hope he hasn't pined for me too much."

"So there is someone," he said in a crestfallen manner. "I absolutely refuse to believe I am the only gentleman who is aware of your many wonderful qualities."

"Max is my dog."

"Do you mean that oversized hairy mongrel who tried to separate me from my leg when I called upon your father?" the duke asked in some astonishment.

"He is rather naughty, but I am exceedingly fond of him."

"I daresay I shall be obliged to grow used to him," the duke conceded, "as well as any other animals you have contrived to assemble around you. Have I cause for hope, my darling?"

She moved a little closer to him. "You were the one who said there was another when I last saw you at the concert."

"I was, of course, talking about Hal."

"Not Lady Westcot?"

He laughed disparagingly. "No! Definitely not Lady Westcot."

"You were in love with her before she married Lord Westcot. Everyone says so."

"I don't say so and never have, and let me tell you something, Minty, if I had loved her, she would not have been permitted to marry Charlie Westcot."

He moved closer to her and drew her into his arms, aware that she shivered slightly with pleasure. "You did tell me at the fair you didn't dislike me. In fact, I recall you said you liked me tolerably well."

Araminta gazed at him lovingly. "I couldn't very well tell you I loved you, could I?"

"You can now."

She sighed. "I love you, Oliver," she whispered, as she gave herself up to his embrace at last.